More Critical Praise for A

"Winkler never glosses over Jamaican deprivation, prejudice, and violence, yet the love of language—and the language of love—somehow conquers all. It's as if P.G. Wodehouse had strolled into the world of Bob Marley. Or as if a more salacious Alexander McCall Smith tangled with the younger, funnier V.S. Naipul. But, truth be told, Winkler sounds like no one but himself . . . A body of work to treasure and trumpet." —*The Independent* (UK)

"Every country (if she's lucky) gets the Mark Twain she deserves, and Winkler is ours, bristling with savage Jamaican wit, heart-stopping compassion, and jaw-dropping humor all at once."
—Marlon James, author of *John Crow's Devil*

"Hilarious, bawdy, vivid, and insightful . . . Winkler is unequivocally unafraid . . . Winkler can ask the big questions without becoming tiresome." —*Caribbean Review of Books*

Praise for *Dog War*

"Winkler applies his wicked sensibility to immigrant experience in Florida . . . He has a fine ear for patois and dialogue, and a love of language that makes bawdy jokes crackle." —*New Yorker*

"A family comedy par excellence, Winkler negotiates the fine line between laughing with and at a character with aplomb . . . Winkler's timing is well honed, and this comedy of cultural and generational clashes hits the right notes nearly every time . . . This is Winkler's first novel to be published in America, but his reputation as a comic novelist precedes him. With *Dog War*, he more than lives up to it."
—*Time Out Chicago* (four stars)

"*Dog War* offers an amusing glance at America through an immigrant's eye, a breezy treat to keep you company on the beach at Montego Bay or, perhaps, your local dog park."
—*Entertainment Weekly*

"*Dog War* has its laugh-out-loud moments, for it is sweetened by Jamaican-patois dialogue from Winkler's homeland and wry, tongue-in-cheek narration . . . [A] delicious comedy of manners." —*Booklist*

"When was the last time you laughed out loud at a book, and I mean the hold-your-sides, near-hysterical-with-joy kind of laughter? *Dog War* is a pitch-perfect and truly uplifting read, wonderfully written with a flourish and an art that is like the best conversation. Winkler is the Prozac of literature, the true feel-good factor we seek in Oprah and the likes. You want to help somebody? . . . Give them *Dog War*, they'll be forever in your debt." —Ken Bruen, author of *The Guards*

"*Dog War* is a delightful satire of Jamaican, and, especially, American life, as funny as a Donald E. Westlake crime caper and as outrageous as John Collier's *His Monkey Wife.*" —*Tampa Tribune*

"An acclaimed comic novelist in his native Jamaica, Winkler makes a long overdue American debut with this laugh riot . . . Winkler's wit, his ear for dialect and the sublime creation that is Precious add up to one howlingly funny book." —*Publishers Weekly*

"Winkler paves every step with delicious laugh-out-loud prose that offers a wide-angled view of Jamaica's culture." —*Jamaica Gleaner*

Praise for *The Lunatic*

"By far the funniest book I've read in a decade, although its ribald atmosphere is sprayed with the pepper-gas of aggressive social satire." —*Washington Post Book World*

"*The Lunatic* is a small masterpiece and should not be missed." —*ForeWord*

"*The Lunatic* is beautiful and insane and unlike any other in its comedy of character and idea, landscape and language; a sensibility that jostles the senses." —Benjamin Weissman, author of *Headless*

"*The Lunatic* is a brilliantly written and outrageous Jamaican fable." —*Jamaica Gleaner*

GOD CARLOS

GOD CARLOS

BY ANTHONY C. WINKLER

AKASHIC
BOOKS

Published by Akashic Books
©2012 Anthony Winkler

ISBN-13: 978-1-61775-139-4
Library of Congress Control Number: 2012939262

First printing

Akashic Books
PO Box 1456
New York, NY 10009
info@akashicbooks.com
www.akashicbooks.com

To Cathy, the treasure of my heart

CHAPTER 1

He was a short brown man who lived in a world some believed was flat while he himself was adamant that it was round. Standing half naked in the gloomy candlelit room, his pantaloons crumpled on the floor, he was explaining his reasoning as to why the world could not be flat to the plump naked whore awaiting him on the sagging wooden bed.

The whore was not interested in the shape of the world or his opinions about it, but by encouraging him to talk she bought time to massage his short, thick cock with the palm oil coated on her thumb and forefinger, making him easier to take. Wise to the ways of men like him, she knew that they took pleasure in hurting her.

As he ranted on passionately about why the world could not be flat, she pretended to listen while she slowly worked the palm oil into the knobby engorged head. He shuddered once as she did this, and she quickly stopped her massaging, knowing that if he discharged now, he would not want to pay her.

"It can't be flat!" he exclaimed, as she pulled him firmly by the cock toward the pink vulva gaping obscenely between her legs.

"No?" she mumbled uncaring, her focus on slipping the thick cock inside her without too much discomfort. She spread her legs wide open, placed both hands on his naked butttocks, and with a powerful thrust, stabbed him inside her with a groan.

He stopped talking about the flat earth and began a vigorous thrusting. He had not had a woman in months, and the fluids that were dammed up inside him had begun to vaporize and affect his head with poisonous humors. He believed that if he left any of them inside him he could develop a fever and possibly get sick, even die. What he was doing to the whore, and what the whore was doing to him was, in his mind, a beneficial draining.

He plunged into her as deep as he could go, feeling her wince under him and hearing her groan, which was good, for it meant she would tap deep into the old fluids and draw them completely out of him. He wanted to last long, believing that the more he could delay his discharge, the better for his health, but the palm oil and the massaging had done their work. Moreover, she was squeezing him like an anaconda snake swallowing prey, making a flexing movement over the head of his entrapped cock that was driving him mad. He exploded with a loud grunt like the bark of a wild animal and pumped the whore with a frenzied energy.

In a moment, it was over. He collapsed atop her with a wheeze of exhaustion.

She pushed him off her bosom abruptly, and with a gyrating movement of her hips, expelled him, glistening and drooling, from between her legs. She glanced over at the table, where he had placed the money, and sat up in bed with a sigh of weariness. He was the fifth man she had taken tonight, and she'd had enough.

"I have climbed the crow's nest of a ship at sea," he said, feeling suddenly vulnerable and weak, "and seen the curve of the earth."

She sat down on a chamber pot, spread her legs, and began to openly wash her pussy, which dribbled disgustingly. He shuddered, for she suddenly seemed ugly and loathsome. It was inconceivable that just a minute ago his loins had been afire for her.

He dressed hurriedly while she sat on the chamber pot and wiped herself with a soiled rag and hummed a song she had learned as a child. From the doorway he threw a defiant, parting shot at her: "No matter what anybody tells you, our world is not flat. It is round."

She did not even look up as he slipped out of the seedy room and closed the door behind him, so engrossed was she in scrubbing between her legs with the absentminded distraction of an artisan cleaning a prized tool.

She only glanced at the table where he'd left the twenty maravedis to be sure he didn't try to steal her money as many men had done before. Under the flickering lamp light, she could make out the pile of copper coins that cast a wavering shadow, small and cylindrically shaped like a turd.

She had the money. That was all that mattered.

She didn't even know his name.

CHAPTER 2

He had a long imposing name, for as a male child of sixteenth-century Spain, he was expected to memorialize dead uncles or cousins or nephews, preserve the identity of his mother's family name, and earn the goodwill of saints by acknowledging them in every recital of his full name.

In all its splendor, his full name was Carlos Antonio Maria Eduardo Garcia de la Cal Fernandez. Uncle Eduardo, his mother's beloved brother, was thereby remembered; Antonio would no doubt catch the eye of powerful St. Anthony; Maria memorialized his mother and pacified the blessed Virgin Mary, mother of God. As for the rest of it, Garcia was a sop to the previous generation on his father's side, and de la Cal simply an embellishment of Fernandez, which was a boring and common name that his mother detested even though it signified her marital bond to his father.

His mother had played with the family name many times now, at the birth of almost every child, and since she'd had sixteen of them, she was able to give full rein to her imagination. Record keeping was sloppy in those days, and a woman who kept birthing children was entitled to indulge her fantasies over their potential greatness, even as she lost most of them to commonplace diseases such as diphtheria and measles almost as fast as she could bring them into the world. Yet with all this vainglory embedded in his name, he was still known to his friends and most others as Carlos.

He was not a big man. European men of his time were not tall, although they had inherited from their fathers a voracious appetite for slaughter that would make up in ferocity what they lacked in size.

Nor was he particularly handsome. His face was misshapen and his features gnomic. His nose and eyes and mouth looked as if they were compressed together in too small a space, like the face of a badly sewn cloth doll. And already, although he was only twenty-five, so fissured and worn from too much sun was his face that it looked older and yellowish like the wrinkled skin on an old chicken's leg.

If he was lucky, he would live another ten years. If he was unlucky, he would be carried off earlier by any of the bacilli passed around by bad hygiene, improperly prepared food, and the general nastiness common to sixteenth-century Europe.

He was, moreover, an unthinking man. Catholicism had been so thoroughly beaten into him as a child by a succession of harsh nuns and priests that he believed nothing that had not been filtered through the prism of his teachings. Whatever his church said he accepted unquestioningly. This rigorous Catholicism had made him a curious mixture of animal carnality and spiritual wistfulness. He was always wishing he were better, but constantly berating himself for being worse. Right now, as he stood on the edge of the street, he was tormented by a relentless guilt over his most recent sin—fornication. Even in the open air, the smell of the whore still lingered in his nostrils. He desperately longed to find a priest or pardoner who would absolve him, for he was conscious that should he die at this moment, his soul would plunge straight to hell.

With this terrible thought on his mind, he stood for a brief moment outside the building in which the whore lived, feeling both sinful and aggrieved by the quickness with which she had dispatched him, and although he tingled with that inexpressible relief men feel after having ejaculated deep inside a woman, he also felt that he had been robbed. For a moment or two, he thought about barging into her room and demanding at least a partial refund.

Twenty maravedis for a blink of her time! For an entire day's work as an able seaman, he made only thirty-three maravedis. He had been inside her for no more than a minute or two—surely she should've charged him only ten maravedis. It was worth no more than that, and he would tell her so. He abruptly turned and headed for the doorway out of which he had just come.

But he stopped before his foot had crossed the threshold.

Many such women had men around them as protectors. Perhaps she had a boyfriend or guardian armed with a sword or a pike. He had been stabbed once, a long time ago, in a barroom brawl in Málaga after just returning from a voyage to Gambia. He had gotten into a fight with another seaman—his first serious fight—and while he flailed his dagger around and screamed curses at his opponent, the other man calmly lunged and stabbed him in the chest. The wound had festered. He had come down with a bad fever and couldn't go to sea for three months. Quibbling with a whore over money was not worth the risk of being stabbed. And with fresh sin on his soul, this was the wrong time to risk being killed.

He sighed heavily, like a horse blowing after hauling a particularly heavy load, and wished that he were a divinity, if only long enough to teach that dirty woman a lesson. It was a fantasy he'd had all his life. Other boys would dream of becoming a bishop or a scholar or a mapmaker. He would dream of being godlike.

It was a dream he shared with no one. In his heart, he knew that it was a sinful dream. Nevertheless, he often fantasized about what he would do to his enemies or to people he hated if only he had godlike powers.

In truth, he had no overt enemies, being a little man who would prefer to retaliate sneakily against anyone who crossed him rather than confront his provoker openly.

But he hated many people, many on sight. Whenever he saw someone in the street who wore a splendid hat or a brocaded coat, he felt hatred. He himself was a poor seafarer who dressed in linen pants and a loosely fitting doublet. He wore a simple pair of goatskin shoes that were thinning in the soles.

It did not seem fair that others should have so much more than he. Had he not been his mother's favorite? Did he not have an immortal soul as worthy of redemption as anyone's? Why should he be dressed in threadbare clothes and leaky shoes while others sashayed past him gleaming with tooled leather and silken splendor? Such contrasts were the work of the devil.

So he took his revenge by wishing upon the splendid one some horrible disease such as the worm that ate you from the inside, crawling out of your limbs, your belly, laying its eggs under your skin or behind your eyeballs. He did not know the name of the disease. He only knew that a friend of his friend Rodrigo knew someone who had had it and who had personally witnessed the suffering it caused. This unfortunate man had signed on with a noa exploring the west coast of Africa and had picked up the worm, perhaps from breathing bad air. If he were a divinity, he would cause such things to happen to the rich. But he was just a man, so he could only dream.

Yet though he had a mad dream of being born divine, he was not mad. He knew the difference between the real world in which he scrounged daily and the dream world to which he occasionally retreated for solace. And standing in the street of Cádiz, Spain, on this Thursday evening of March 8, 1520, he knew that he had to quickly find a place to sleep. With only forty maravedis left to his name, he also needed to find a ship that would hire him on as a seaman.

When he had first stepped into the whore's room, he had hoped that she would like him well enough to ask him to spend the night. Such a wonderful thing had happened to Manuel a year ago, or so his shipmate had boasted. But such things never happened to him.

He sighed again. He was standing on a narrow dirt side street near the waterfront, and the shadows that stretched out all around him foretold the falling night. He could smell the tang of saltwater in the breeze. Over the roof of a distant building across the street, he could glimpse the masts of tied-up ships. He knew what he had to do, but he stood there outside the whore's lodgings glancing around as if he were lost.

He was not lost. He was in Cádiz. But he was befuddled and nearly penniless. All he had to his credit was his serpentine name—Carlos Antonio Maria Eduardo Garcia de la Cal Fernandez.

Cádiz, already an old city even in the sixteenth century, having been founded by the Phoenicians in 1000 BC, lay at the center of the exploratory movement

ever since Columbus had made his historic voyage to
the New World. Only a few months earlier, Magellan
had set out to sea on the first attempt to sail completely around the world. With Charles V sitting on
the throne, Spain was prosperous and powerful. Her
reach extended to the Netherlands, Luxembourg, Ar-
tois, and Franche-Comté, Aragón, Navarre, Granada,
Naples, Sicily, Sardinia, and Spanish America. The
Jews had been expelled almost thirty years earlier, and
the suppression of the remaining Muslims had begun
with Isabella's decree of the 12th of February, 1502,
which separated all Muslim males under the age of
fourteen and all females under the age of twelve from
their families and turned them over to the church to
be brought up as Christians. It would spark another
interval of bloodletting in the name of God—a favorite pastime of Europeans.

None of this was known to him, however, for he
barely knew how to read, and there were no newspa-
pers or magazines to tell him what was happening in
the world. Even so, it is unlikely that he would've been
interested. He did not have a mind for current events.
He was only interested in keeping his belly full and finding someplace warm to spend cold nights. He did not
care about causes or principles. He knew that the world
was round, for he had glimpsed its curvature from the
crow's nest of a ship sailing the deep sea, but he did not
care whether or not anyone actually proved it.

As he stood on the street, the stench of raw sewage

rose up all around him and made his eyes run. It was evening and the citizens of Cádiz were emptying their chamber pots in the street, leaving a ghastly, fetid trail of freshly deposited excrement whose malodorous vapors gave off a poisonous stench.

Looking around him at the dingy shops and unreinforced masonry houses, smelling the pungent refuse splattered all over the rutted dirt road still muddy and drooling with runoff from the recent rains, he remembered again why he loved the sea, why he could not abide land and land-bound people. It was the stench of land that he abhorred, the perpetual miasma that arose from it. Wherever people herded together in great numbers, they gave off a collective stink that bedaubed even the breeze. Everything they touched, everything they brushed against, absorbed their stench. The land, the plants, the very animals became impregnated with their stink.

At sea a boat had its stink spots too, but it was a localized stench like a laborer's armpits that one could walk away from. Moreover, the sea breezes were natural cleansers that would sweep away any miasmatic buildup and freshen both man and vessel with the delicate aroma of saltwater.

When the sea was kittenish with him, when his ship was scudding along in a following breeze and the workload easy, he would feel light-headed with exhilaration and joy and wonder how any man with a heart could live anywhere else.

But he was a hardened enough seaman to know that the ocean was fickle and unforgiving. He had already suffered shipwreck. He had lost crewmates on other voyages. Once, after a hurricane, he had drifted clinging to flotsam for eight hours before another ship happened by and saved his life.

So he had no illusions about the sea. It was not a romance for him. All he knew was that land was dirty and stank and was filled with strange people and customs that could drive a man mad and goad him to the deadly sins of covetousness and envy. The sea, on the other hand, was clean and sweet smelling like a freshly bathed and powdered woman.

He was eager and ready to go to sea again, to escape the nasty clutch of land. If he could find a ship about to sail and sign on, perhaps the master would allow him to sleep on the deck, and he wouldn't have to pay a night's lodging. If that did not happen, and if the cheaper inns were full, he would have to sleep on the streets. He had done that many times before. He did not want to do it tonight, for at this time of the year, the night chill could bite down to the very bone.

He set off toward the waterfront, headed for the tangle of masts looming above the rooflines of the surrounding buildings. As he crossed the street, he took care, like everyone else around him, to step cautiously around the piles of excrement that mounded everywhere in his path like poisonous toadstools.

Madre de Dios, he asked himself, was there a more wretched place on this earth than the infernal land?

CHAPTER 3

ádiz is nestled on the tip of an isthmus strate-
gically located on the Atlantic Ocean near the
narrow mouth of the Mediterranean Sea. Not far
away, across the Straits of Gibraltar, looms the dark
forehead of vast Africa with its ancient lands of Algeria, Morocco, Tunisia—kingdoms once populated
by Berbers, a motley Afro-Asiatic people who sprang
from an unknown origin and covered caves with painted images dating back to 6500 BC Next to Algeria on
the simian brow of Africa lies Morocco, another ancient kingdom repeatedly overrun by invaders, from
the Phoenicians of the twelfth century BC and later
the Carthaginians, the Romans, and the Vandals—all
of these, kingdoms that came and went on the world
stage like surging swarms of locusts.

Carlos knew about none of this history though
its teachings and lessons had been subtly imprinted
on his soul and informed his outlook in ways that he
could only act out but did not understand. He was
barely able to read, having had only three years of
schooling at the hands of an overworked village priest
who was ahead of his time in his belief in public edu-
cation. What Carlos was proudest of was that he had

learned to write his first name in a shaky cursive hand
and did not, like most of his shipmates, have to mark
an imbecilic X when he signed up to work on a ship.

On his way to the quay, he encountered a beggar
whom bone disease had twisted into a misshapen car-
icature of the human body, and desiring God's mercy
after his sinful encounter with the whore, Carlos dug
deep into his pocket and fished out a single maravedi,
which he flipped to the wretched man, drawing peals
of extravagant blessings that God would surely not
overlook.

He was whistling merrily when he finally came to
the waterfront. The smell of fish assailed his nose and,
as he turned a corner, a tangle of masts and rigging
hung like an enormous spiderweb above ships tied up
abeam on the quay. A gale churning over the Atlantic
had sent many vessels scurrying into Cádiz as a haven
from the storm, where they now bobbed disheveled
and weather beaten.

Scattered over the quay was a familiar ensemble of
castaways, adventurers, ship jumpers, whores, scav-
engers, cutthroats, pickpockets, and foreigners—the
same found in dirty waterfronts all over this rounded
earth. Some scruffy characters ambled aimlessly past
the ships; others slouched against the stained walls
of stone warehouses, staring blurrily at memories of
distant shores or long-lost sweethearts left behind in
faraway homelands. Here and there men skulked in
the shadows, scanning every stranger with a vague

predatory curiosity. Some seamen huddled together in boisterous discussion about voyages and adventures they had survived. On a few of the tied-up ships, sailors squatted on deck splicing ropes or patching sails. One grommet was cleaning the foredeck of a noa with soapstone. Trolling the banks of the quay for customers were a couple of painted, aged whores. Beyond the ships and the human jetsam unfurled the open ocean, crinkled and gray in the distance, and far out to sea Carlos could glimpse an ominously dark squall line that made a sailor give thanks for solid land underfoot.

He walked slowly down the quay, eyeing the lashed-together vessels, appraising each one with a practiced eye. He passed frigates, dismissing out of hand those equipped with oars. An impatient master who found himself on a windless sea would have his men break their backs with rowing. For similar reasons, he turned up his nose at an opulent-looking brigantine and passed up several coastal barks. He had a personal distaste for hybrid vessels that combined sails with oars. Such ships were usually not only ungainly under sail, but nearly impossible to row.

He strolled past a weather-beaten noa, looming bulky over the neighboring vessels, her high forecastle and raised quarterdeck giving her a top-heavy profile.

A noa was not a bad ship. Christopher Columbus himself, Admiral of the Ocean Sea, dead these past fourteen years now, God rest his soul, had chosen a noa—the famed *Santa Maria*—for his flagship. Yet

Carlos still preferred a vessel that did not brandish a broad beam and high freeboard at capricious seas. Such a vessel was wonderful for running before a following wind but handled poorly to windward.

What he wanted was to find a sturdy sailer such as a caravel, particularly one headed for the New World. He had been to Africa. He had scoured the length and breadth of the Mediterranean, sailing as far away as Crete. He was tired of these old seas and their nasty ports.

On waterfronts all over the Mediterranean and Atlantic the talk was of the New World and the strange, exotic people who lived in it. Carlos had never seen one of these creatures himself, but he'd heard many drunken exaggerations about them. The women, it was said, walked around naked as the day they were born and gave freely of their affections to strangers. One sailor who claimed his cousin's brother-in-law had shipped on the second voyage of discovery with the Admiral of the Ocean Sea himself swore that there were so many lovely available women that the intemperate man could easily kill himself with too much lovemaking.

He was musing quietly to himself about sailing to an exotic land where all the woman were lovely and willing when he heard a voice hailing him. One of the blessed saints had heard his prayers, perhaps St. Anthony, and answered them, for right before him was a caravel whose low rakish waterline bespoke a ship loaded and ready for sea. Painted on her bow was her name, *Santa Inez*.

From her raised quarterdeck, a man in his later years, who carried himself with the authority of a master, was calling him.

"I said, are you looking for a ship?"

At first, Carlos admitted nothing. He had learned a long time ago that in a new situation it was better to listen than to talk. So he was cryptic and noncommittal in his replies, irritating the stranger, who said he was from Mallorca. He said he was master of this ship, which would sail tomorrow for the New World, but he was shorthanded because unexpected death had visited his crew. If he was an experienced sailor looking for a ship, here was opportunity.

"What's your name?" the stranger asked.

"Carlos."

"I am Alonso de la Serena, and this is my ship," the stranger said, pounding the railing with his knuckles like a shopkeeper boasting about a new counter.

"Where are you bound?" Carlos asked diffidently.

"To Jamaica, where there are fortunes waiting to be made. Gold so plentiful that it washes down rivers like gravel. Labor so cheap that it costs a man nothing to put in a crop. Feed the natives, and they work like mules. A climate so beneficent that men live to be seventy and eighty years old without infirmity of mind or body because the air is so sweet and the nights so

mild. It is a paradise that awaits us only a month's sail
away."

Carlos glanced at the ship, noting the neatness of
the ropes and the cleanliness of the deck. He swept
his eye over the main mast and noticed the tight furl
of the sails. She was a three-masted lateener that bore
the influence of Portuguese shipwrights, but she had
been rerigged to fly a square sail, her lateen yards removed. Alonso anticipated his query.

"The wind will be behind us for most of the voyage.
On the return, if we foolishly decide to leave paradise,
we will ride the westerlies back to Spain. A lateen
sail is difficult for running. It is the same change that
Christopher Columbus made to his vessel."

Carlos knew well the deficiencies of the lateen sail.
He remembered the nightmare of steering a lateen-
rigged frigate bound from Tangier for the west coast
of Africa. The ship yawed badly, and with every little
shift of the wind, the lateen had to be readjusted,
which meant lowering the sail and hoisting it again
on the other side of the main mast. Five men had to
do this in the darkness with a lumpy following sea
pounding them astern and the light from the three-
quarter moon barely enough to illuminate the rigging.
That was one of the worst nights he'd ever spent on
a ship since he took to sea as a grommet of eleven—
and it was all because of an unsuitable lateen sail. The
Mallorcan was truly a seaman.

The discussion veered to the particulars. It was

the particulars that drove sailors mad on a long voy-age, the little pinpricks that the master would enforce at sea. Sometimes a man who was harsh in port turned into a mild and friendly master once the ship was un-derway. But more often than not, it was the opposite that was true—the man who was gentle when his feet were on land became a demon at sea. One had no way to predict this change, but Carlos had a theory. He had found that capricious and harsh masters showed their true underside in port when questioned on one issue: the sleeping arrangements permitted aboard ship.

"Where do you allow your men to sleep, señor," he asked mildly, fixing the older man with a careful stare.

"Anywhere they like," came the crisp reply, "so long as their presence does not interfere with the smooth running of the ship."

"On deck, at nights?"

"Certainly, on deck. But I warn every man to lash himself down with rope so he won't be washed over-board."

"You do not insist that the men sleep below?"

"It is an oven sometimes below deck," de la Serena said candidly. "No man should be asked to sleep in an oven."

Carlos tried to read the craggy face before him, to fathom its temperament, its truthfulness. De la Serena returned his stare openly, and for a brief moment the two of them looked at each other deeply like lovers.

Then Carlos, feeling uncomfortable, turned away with a casual shrug.

He did not understand how anyone could be born on Mallorca—one of the Baeleric Islands, consisting of eleven islets and four larger islands, none of which Carlos particularly liked, probably because he had visited them only during stormy seas when his ship was in danger of floundering. He thought the island barren and inhospitable, suitable with its ironbound shoreline as a rookery for sea birds.

De la Serena asked a series of nautical questions, to test Carlos's seamanship, and the Spaniard answered with an offhanded nonchalance that bespoke his experience. The older man knew a sailor when he saw one. Carlos knew the names of all the kinds of vessels tied up around them. He had strong opinions on the handling differences between a lateen sail and square rigging. Like most seamen of the day, he was filled with suspicions and had stories to tell about how some talisman had saved his life. But more importantly, to de la Serena at least, was that he bargained hard for the little comforts that true seamen loved to have around them—liberal run of the ship, for example—asking questions about the cook and the types of meals that would be served.

It remained only for Carlos to pass one more test, and de la Serena, who had already decided to sign him on, asked him to shimmy up the main mast and climb into the crow's nest. The *Santa Inez*, like all vessels of her day, was without ratlines, which had not yet been invented, and reaching her crow's nest required a seaman's agility and strength.

Carlos walked over to the main mast, gripped a halyard, leaped onto the mast, and propelled himself up, using his hands and feet to clasp the wood. In a blink, he was in the crow's nest and pretending to be scanning the horizon.

"Come down and sign the papers," de la Serena invited.

Carlos slid down the mast. "I have nowhere to sleep tonight," he began, but de la Serena cut him short.

"Sleep aboard ship," he said, heading below for the papers.

A few minutes later, the mostly ritualistic signing was complete, and Carlos got the opportunity to show off his cursive signature with all its elaborate curlicues. His contract said that until the *Santa Inez* returned to Cádiz, Carlos was bound to service aboard her at one thousand maravedis per month. It was not much, but it was a little more than Carlos had earned on his last ship.

De la Serena opened a bottle of wine and they drank a goblet each and shared some bread. Other than the two of them and a cabin boy named Pedro who mostly stayed out of sight, the ship was deserted, the crew having gone carousing for what might be the last night ashore for many weeks. With a little wine under his belt, de la Serena became very talkative, and the two men sat on deck and chatted about the Indies while a grainy darkness settled over Cádiz.

Carlos was content. He listened sleepily to the other man's rambling, casting an occasional eye at the whores prowling the shadows and weighing his chances of sweet-talking one of them into giving him a free sample.

Such a thing had never happened to him, but a long time ago, he had shipped out with a man from Albacete who swore that it had happened to his cousin in Perpignan, France, during a layover of five days while a bitter storm raged over the Mediterranean. It was a miraculous interlude that his cousin had enjoyed with the whore, all done freely and with affection. In fact, when the bad weather lifted and the time to sail again had come, the whore handed him a sackful of money and begged him to jump ship and live with her. Such a thing had never happened to Carlos, yet he was hopeful.

Some few hours later, he curled up in a corner of the deck and went to sleep. De la Serena retreated to his quarters below. Like many ships of her time, the *Santa Inez* had only a single private compartment, which belonged to the master. Everyone else aboard shared the common areas of the ship as living space.

Carlos fell into a deep sleep as a crescent moon leaked a soft saffron light over the minarets of Cádiz erected in the eighth century by Moor invaders.

Over the centuries, all of Spain had been a bloody battleground between Christianity and Islam, and everywhere on this ancient land vestiges marking the dominance of one creed over the other lingered. The bulbed towers soared over the smaller buildings of the sleeping city like stalks of giant tulips, and it required only a little imagination to hear the bleat of a muezzin calling the Islamic faithful to prayer. But that custom was no longer observed, Alfonso the Wise, king of Leon and Castile, having driven the Moors out of Cádiz in the early thirteenth century, restoring Christianity.

None of this was known to Carlos, who, though he was not an innocent, always slept soundly, for a seaman learned to sleep anywhere and anytime when he was tired. And today, a long and trying day by his own calculation, had been exhausting. So although the deck was hard and the wood cold against his bones, he was asleep almost as quickly as his head touched the floor.

CHAPTER 4

Carlos was jolted from the blurriness of a dream by what he thought were squabbling birds. But then from the rear of the ship he heard a coarse male voice booming and realized that he had been awakened by a noisy quarrel.

Raising his head carefully to peep over the deck railing, he saw a knot of four women on the quay, one old and three young, gesturing angrily and screaming at the ship. On the quarterdeck de la Serena stood hurling insults back at them.

"You are an old man, an unwell man! It is madness to go to sea in your condition. Come home, Alonso. Give up this rashness. Accept God's will and be thankful!"

"There is nothing wrong with me that a long voyage won't cure!" de la Serena thundered.

"Papa! I miss you already! I beg of you, return home with us," one of the young woman bleated pitifully.

"Don't worry," de la Serena bellowed back with heavy sarcasm, "your dowry is safe. I have made arrangements on your behalf. You will not be deprived of one maravedi."

"Papa, it's not the money. It's you."

"And how long did your mother rehearse you in that touching speech?" de la Serena sneered.

Crewmen who had returned late began to emerge from different parts of the ship, rubbing their eyes and yawning at the commotion. A few of them leaned against the railings, grinning and spitting.

The row waged on, with the women spilling tears and wailing like they were demented while de la Serena blasted them from the quarterdeck with a string of rebuttal oaths. The older woman called on the Virgin Mary to bear witness to how a hard-hearted husband and father was deserting his family in their greatest hour of need and fleeing like a young *caballero* to the so-called New World.

"There's nothing new about it!" shrieked the wife. "It is just as old as our world. You will die there and be buried an old man unmourned among strangers. Your bones will be eaten by wild dogs. No grandchildren will ever put flowers on your grave."

"Papa, stay with us. Don't leave us here alone!"

"I curse this ship, this *Santa Inez*. If it takes my husband from me, may it be cursed with bad weather and sea serpents! May the Holy Virgin raise her hand against this vessel that would separate a husband and father from his wife and daughters."

On hearing this malediction against their ship, some sailors began to surlily mutter among themselves, and one or two, as if they could stand to hear no more, drifted away below deck or stepped onto the quay and wandered off out of earshot.

"We sail with the tide," de la Serena called after two of the men as they left. They waved in dismissive acknowledgment and continued strolling down the quay without looking back.

"When did you sign on?" an older sailor who spoke with the accent of an Andalusian asked Carlos.

"Last night," Carlos replied. "I am Carlos Antonio Maria Eduardo Garcia de la Cal Fernandez."

He did not know why he gave his full name except that he felt like it. The old man acknowledged him with a little nod and muttered, after spitting elaborately over the side and watching his spittle float away, "My name is Hernandez Medina. I do not like it when women curse a ship before she sails. It brings the worst kind of bad luck."

"So I have heard," Carlos responded indifferently.

Another man joined them. "Hernandez, did you hear what she said? She has put a curse on our ship."

"That is what we were just talking about. I do not like this."

"I will not sail on this ship unless the curse is taken back," the man muttered darkly, walking off.

"I'd better tell the captain about this," Hernandez said with a sigh. "We're already shorthanded."

He scurried across the deck and conferred with the captain while the women continued to wail at the ship, their voices rising in a shriller stridency. After some back-and-forth whispering between the two men, de la Serena, with obvious reluctance, crossed the gangplank and waded among the women, pleading with them in a low voice as they sniffled and wept and touched his clothing as though to keep him land bound. Huddled closely together, the group drifted away, still chattering animatedly with each other.

"It is often like this," old Hernandez intoned solemnly, appearing at Carlos's side. "The man wishes to leave because his heart belongs to the sea, and the women try to bind him to the land."

"But is he sick?" Carlos pressed.

"He is sick of land life," Hernandez said dryly. "He longs for the sea. He wants to have something in the New World named after him. It is his passion."

"What does he want to be named after him?"

Hernandez shrugged. "A river, a mountain, a town, an estuary, a bay—anything that will outlast a man and give him some remembrance. Everything in Spain is already named. Many things are still unnamed in the New World."

"That is why he's going to Jamaica?"

"That is why he's going to Jamaica."

And the seaman expertly sent a wad of spit arcing over the deck of the *Santa Inez* where it plopped like a pebble in the murky sea coiling tidal threads around the barnacled pilings of the quay.

Moving like one body, de la Serena and his huddled family had drifted off to a shaded spot under the

eaves of a warehouse, where they were intensely ne-
gotiating his departure in hugger-mugger whispering.

At two that afternoon, the *Santa Inez* cast off her shore-
lines, picked a path through the thinning throng
of ships, many of which had departed earlier, and
kedged her way into the harbor. She rode the ebb tide
until she caught a sea breeze that billowed out her
mainmast square sail and bonnet and drove her into
the Atlantic.

Except for a few bystanders who watched her
shove off with mild curiosity, no one who loved her
was on the quay to wave goodbye. Whatever de la Serena had said to his family was enough, for his wife
and daughters had departed hours ago, trailing behind them a muffled weeping. Once clear of the harbor, the *Santa Inez* hoisted her foremast square sail and
was soon spanking briskly along to a quartering wind.

To a man, her crew was Spanish and Catholic, a
short race of men resembling Carlos in build and complexion, stumpy and thick like drought-stunted trees.
She had left port shorthanded, the curses called down
on her by de la Serena's wife having cost her five crew,
who simply walked away rather than sail on a vessel that might have displeased the Virgin Mary. She
should have had a complement of at least twenty-five.
Instead, her crew numbered only twenty, not counting de la Serena. They were sailing a vessel of some
sixty tons—calculated in storage capacity for casks of

wine, *toneladas*, as was the prevailing measure of the day. She was some seventy feet long with a twenty-five-foot beam and nine feet deep amidships.

Behind her, the Iberian Peninsula looked like a ravenous millipede erupting out of the body of continental Europe to sink its teeth into the brow of Africa. Seeing this, however, required a perspective aloft that sailors of that time did not have except in their dreams. Trapped at sea level, they could see only the gentle waves splashing against the hull of their ship; off the port side, the immensities of Africa; and astern, Cádiz wobbling low on the horizon.

The *Santa Inez* was steering southwest, a course that would take her near the Canary Islands. This passage between Spain and the Canaries had already become the traditional route to the New World based on the prevailing winds. It was usually a rough passage, its Spanish nickname being then el Golfo de las Yeguas—the Sea of the Mares—for the many brood mares that had died while being shipped to the Canaries. But as the Admiral had shown, it was a necessary passage to catch the northeast trades to the New World.

For now, the weather was mild, the seas gently rolling.

It is the truism of seafarers that every sailor deals in his own way with a new voyage. Some men become morose and moody, putting on a sullen face until they get accustomed to the rhythm of their sea schedule.

Others are cheerful and outgoing, laughing at the least joke, ecstatically happy to be away from land where they had cross wives, demanding girlfriends, or were burdened with debts they could not repay. For Carlos, the first days at sea were always days of withdrawal.

Long experience had taught Carlos that if he remained quiet and kept his own counsel, eventually the voyage ahead and the ensuing days of uncertainty and tedium would gradually seem natural. So he kept to himself and did not speak unless someone spoke to him first or unless it was absolutely necessary. For the first days, when he was off duty, he sat by himself on deck near the bow where he could idly watch the occasional dolphins that swam playfully alongside.

Shortly after the ship cleared Cádiz and hit the open sea, de la Serena set the watch schedule. He divided the watch into four-hour shifts, rotating them among the various seamen so that no one would be stuck permanently with the dog watch—from midnight to four a.m.

Like most mariners of his day, de la Serena was navigating by dead reckoning, which required keeping track of time. A sailor was therefore named on every watch to promptly turn over the ampoletta—the sand clock—when the sand ran out every half an hour. Knowing how many hours ago he had departed port, and estimating the speed of his ship, allowed a master a fairly accurate estimate of his latitude. Determining longitude, however, required a good chronometer that would not be invented until 1735 by John Harrison, an English carpenter.

Living in a speck of time over a hundred years earlier than Harrison, Carlos was not concerned with the ship's position, but was focused, instead, on making the adjustment to being again at sea. The ship under his feet seemed sturdy and solid. He was being fed one meal daily prepared by a cook in the open fire box in the bow of the ship. Although he lay each night on the hard deck, hugging himself for warmth, he slept soundly, waking only once to relieve himself over the side. With no bathroom aboard, the *Santa Inez*, particularly in the mornings, dragged behind her long, stringy trails of waterlogged excrement like the tentacles of an enormous jellyfish.

It would take some eight days to raise the Canary Islands. By then Carlos had gone through his transition and settled into his maritime self. He became friendlier and exchanged casual chats with other crewmen. De la Serena asked him if he would take his turn at the helm, which was flattering to his seamanship, and Carlos reluctantly agreed.

He did not like to man the helm, for the tiller that controlled the rudder was below deck, and the helmsman, having no view of either the sails or the sea, had to steer only by compass and the feel of the ship, which required great skill.

If the helmsman veered off course or miscalculated the roll of the ship or failed to anticipate the vessel's reaction to a particularly heavy wave, the officer on deck, who was supposed to be his eyes and ears, would yell at him and expose him to ridicule. A clumsy helmsman drew the wrath of his fellow seamen, especially if his insensitive touch on the tiller caused the vessel to yaw and spill the wind from her sails, requiring the labor of retrimming. Such incidents often led to bitter words, even open fights.

Carlos did his best to avoid fights on a ship at sea. Crewmen had a way of disappearing after bitter quarreling. It was an easy thing to do at night, bump a man overboard and send him tumbling into the dark sea. He would scream and cry for help, but with most of the ship asleep—and if the winds were favorable—no one would hear him.

Carlos thought such a death horrible beyond telling. It was so ghastly that even thinking about it made him shudder. You could stay afloat for hours, watching the ship ghost away on the horizon, oblivious to your screams. He could only imagine the heart-stopping terror of being abandoned in dark, open water.

Yet he had done exactly that to a Frenchman, who had done the same thing to Carlos's best friend and shipmate. And he felt no remorse because he had long been absolved of that sin.

It had happened on a voyage to Pátrai in the Ionian Sea. The ship, a tubby Portuguese vessel, was overloaded with wine casks with his friend Juan Morales, a boy from Oviedo, at the helm. It was impossible to hold her on a straight course, and several times she yawed badly, spilling water over her side and drenching the watch on deck. Juan was relieved from the helm, and when he appeared from the steering hole, the Frenchman ridiculed him loudly before everyone present. The boy defended himself heatedly, and harsh words were exchanged. Several days later, when the boy was on dog watch, he suddenly disappeared. No one ever saw him again.

There was such hot-blooded muttering among the Spanish crewmen that the captain, an indifferent Portuguese, had to interrogate the Frenchman, who had also been on duty that night but who passionately denied having anything to do with the boy's disappearance. Yet later, he was heard bragging among his friends about what he did and would do again to any dirty Spaniard who got in his way.

A few nights later, during a gale, Carlos surprised the Frenchman leaning carelessly against the railing of the quarterdeck. It took just a quick shove to send him flying into the sea. Only Carlos heard the one burbling cry for help the man was able to make before a wave shattered over his head and swept him under.

For the rest of that voyage, Carlos made sure that no one came near him at night, and he carried a dagger openly as a warning to any friend of the Frenchman. He also lived fearfully with the mortal sin of murder on his soul until he was able to return to Spain and buy absolution from a roaming pardoner.

On this voyage, Carlos vowed hard to get along with everyone, to offer no jest at another's expense, to avoid all arguments no matter what the topic, and to keep to himself as his own company. He would be pleasant to everyone, but share no intimacies with any of his shipmates. And when he was at the helm, he did his best to hold the ship on a steady course, so those who were on deck would not be exposed to the sea or lose their footing because of the roll of the ship. He had a steady hand and a good feel for the sea, and he would give no one reason to criticize his helmsmanship.

It was a promising beginning to this voyage, also, that he had been having many dreams since the ship sailed. He slept in stretches of four hours between watches, and he dreamed mainly of women. And when he awoke, his limbs would ache from sleeping on the hard decking, his cock would be stiff, and his cheeks would be damp with dew.

Yet the first thing he did on awakening, after his cock had gone down, was to say a prayer to St. Anthony, begging his protection against the perils of the seafarer. He believed that St. Anthony would understand that a man at sea must dream of women, and that no matter how much piety he had in his heart, there was no preventing this lust. It was the price mortal flesh had to pay for being molded into a man.

CHAPTER 5

Spaniards of the sixteenth century practiced an autonomic Catholicism that was as much a part of them as breathing. Carlos was a typical example—instinctively submissive to religious authority and one who would never gainsay even a lowly village priest. That he was a sinful man he freely admitted, and as soon as the piquancy of fresh sin had waned, he quickly went to confession and did penance to atone for his wrongdoing.

With a nearly unimaginable number of ways to commit mortal sin that could damn a soul for eternity, the sixteenth-century Catholic would have been utterly miserable but for the important ritual of confession. According to church doctrine, sin occurred not only in deed, but also in thought. Making love to a woman out of wedlock was the sin of fornication; merely dreaming about doing it was the sin of lust. Since most people cannot control their thoughts or their dreams, virtually every Catholic of sixteenth-century Spain must have felt the day-to-day prick of mortal sin and possible damnation.

But if the definition of sin was so broad as to be inescapable, the remedy was just as easily available.

A Catholic of the sixteenth century was taught by the church that satisfying a particular set of rituals always yielded a predictable result. Going to confession cleansed the soul of sin. Reciting a certain prayer guaranteed the release of a loved one's soul from the tormenting fires of Purgatory. Saying a certain sequence of prayers to the Virgin Mary made her intercede on your behalf with Jesus, her only begotten son. The faithful who obeyed Catholic doctrine and practiced the rituals of Mother Church fully expected to be saved.

As the *Santa Inez* rode the northeast trades and put the Canary island of La Gomera astern, virtually every sailor aboard her was confident that if he didn't reach the New World, he would at least get to heaven.

With the religious beliefs of her crew so homogenous, it was inconceivable that the *Santa Inez* would not include some Catholic liturgy in her running. Like many ships of her time, she began and ended every day with a prayer.

Led by de la Serena, two traditional praying intervals were observed—the *tierce* between eight and nine a.m., and the *compline* between six and nine p.m.—during which the crew recited the Paternoster and the Ave Maria. On many ships, prayers were said every half an hour, but de la Serena was not that devout. Twice a day was enough for his ship. The only other prayers he led were those suggested by circumstances.

So, if the seas were rough, he would pray for calm. If it was a windless day, he would pray for breeze. If a seaman was ill, he would pray for him to recover. If a pump went bad, he would pray for it to be fixed.

Most of these prayers were directed to God the Father, but some were meant for God the Son, some for God the Holy Ghost and others for the Virgin Mary. From long acquaintance, this odd pantheon, which an unbeliever might have found bizarre, made perfect sense to the men, many of whom, feeling vulnerable in a small vessel on an endless sea, found the recital of a daily liturgy to one God subdivided into three personas oddly comforting.

The *Santa Inez* would be at sea anywhere between twenty-eight and thirty-six days—depending on the winds—and cover a distance of some three thousand miles. The sailors themselves thought the journey much shorter, for it was the prevailing belief among mariners of the times that the circumference of the earth was 25 percent smaller that it actually was, a mistake caused by miscalculation of the length of a degree.

Columbus believed that a degree of longitude was forty-five nautical miles long instead of the true distance of sixty. Centuries ago, before the coming of Christ, the Greek mathematician Eratosthenes, with amazing accuracy, had estimated a degree to be 59.5 nautical miles.

But as they set out on their voyages of exploration, navigators of the fifteenth century deliberately
used the smaller estimate because it made their voyages look shorter and therefore less risky. Columbus,
for example, calculated the distance between the Canary Islands and Japan to be 2,400 nautical miles. In
fact, it was over four times that length. But a seafarer
seeking funding for an exploratory trip to Japan—or
Cipangu, as Japan was then known—found it easier to
raise money if Japan was closer.

The ship had settled into her rhythm, the watches
changing smoothly, the daily upkeep required aboard
a sailing vessel being performed so well that the ac-
tions of the crew seemed rehearsed. During every
watch, the crew was responsible for keeping the decks
clean, swabbing them down with buckets of seawater,
and sweeping them with besoms, which were brooms
made of twigs.

A sailing vessel of that era required constant ad-
justments to her halyards, which held up her sails
and yards, and her shrouds, which held her masts in
place. Rope would stretch or become worn in spots
that had to be rerigged with chafing gear. Sails had to
be trimmed and braces adjusted.

Every hour on the hour the helmsman was freed
from his imprisonment in the steering box, where he
was confined behind four walls. At the end of every
stint of steering, Carlos was always grateful for relief

and would briefly retreat to his customary spot near the bow and sit there for a few minutes, reveling in the clean vistas of blue sky and open sea.

By the second week at sea, a sporadic camaraderie had sprung up among the men and some of the crew had formed friendships. Carlos exchanged pleasantries with everyone he met during the changes of the shifts or with the crewmen on his watch. But he still mainly kept to himself, although in the late evenings just before the sun went down, he would occasionally sit with the other men and listen to their discussions about the New World.

One man, a loudmouthed veteran of many voyages named Miguel de Morales, had been to the New World once before and had many stories to tell about the women. It was true, he solemnly told a ring of raptly listening men, that the women went about naked with no sense of shame or modesty and that they were exceedingly friendly with their visitors from overseas, whom they regarded as gods.

Carlos started when the man said this and asked, "As gods, you say?"

A few of the men who were unaccustomed to Carlos asking questions looked quizzically at him as if they were surprised to discover that he could speak.

"As gods," de Morales repeated firmly. "One of their prophets was said to have foretold our coming."

"But don't the Indian men object to their women being friendly with strangers?" a sailor asked.

De Morales chuckled. "Most of the time they don't care, and if they did care, what could they do? They're cowards, these Indian men. And they're ignorant. One of them cut himself on my sword by grabbing its blade."

"Why did he do such a foolish thing?" another sailor wondered.

"Because he'd never seen iron before. He did not know that a sword could cut him."

"Truly, that is ignorance," a sailor who seldom spoke muttered.

"Six well-armed Spaniards would be more than a match for a hundred Indians," de Morales said cockily.

It was beginning to get dark, and lights were winking on throughout the ship.

At sea, there are no gradients to nightfall. In the featureless tundra of empty waves that stretches from horizon to horizon, darkness falls with the uniformity of dew, suffusing the sea in an unvarying intensity. The men watched quietly as the night relentlessly possessed the ocean and their small ship.

"There is one thing about the Indians," de Morales said thoughtfully, breaking the silence, "but it is a little thing. After you have lain with one of the women, it is likely that you will receive a boil on your organ. It is a small sore, but a harmless one that soon goes away. When I was last in the Indies, some years ago, I received a sore that went away. After that, I received no more. It is a strange thing. A man told me that the cause was the first mingling of unfamiliar humors."

The *Santa Inez* was ghosting along to a slacking breeze, for at sea the wind usually dies down with the coming of night. Sailors who had the eleven o'clock watch wandered off to find a favorite spot to sleep.

"I don't think this boil is such a harmless thing," old Hernandez said.

"I have had no further trouble with it," de Morales replied coolly. "It is nothing."

"It would be wonderful to be regarded as a god," Carlos said dreamily.

"Only if you are one," Hernandez said after a moment of thought. "Otherwise you will be a disappointment."

The cabin boy named Pedro, who came from a village in the foothills of the Pyrénées, chuckled. "I wonder what they would do to a man they found out was only a man and not a god."

"Perhaps they would kill him," old Hernandez said.

"These Indians do not kill men easily," proclaimed de Morales. "Their weapons are suitable for fish, but not for killing men."

"I think I would make a wonderful god," Carlos blurted out without thinking, carried away by his fantasy.

The men looked at him as if they could not believe their ears. De Morales guffawed. Pedro grinned but not in an unfriendly way. Old Hernandez made a tutting sound like a disapproving aunt.

"Of course," Carlos amended quickly, "it is an impossible thing. But if I were born a god, I would be a good one."

"That is impious," old Hernandez scolded gently. "Men at sea must not think such things."

"I think I would be a good god too," the boy Pedro gushed.

"I would make a better devil," said a taciturn sailor who sat on the edge of the group listening, but up to now had put in no opinion.

A few of the men chuckled.

"It is not a laughing matter," old Hernandez said. "When we are at sea, we must not vex God, or He will send us sea monsters or bad weather."

An uneasy silence fell over the men. It was broken by de Morales.

"God Carlos," he sneered. "That is your name, isn't it?"

Carlos's face became hard, his voice thin and sharp like a freshly stropped razor. "Carlos Antonio Maria Eduardo Garcia de la Cal Fernandez," he said coldly. "What of it, señor?"

"There will never be a God Carlos," de Morales said scornfully. "It is too funny to even think of."

"This discussion has gone too far," old Hernandez interposed quickly. "We must speak of brighter things."

Carlos stood up, still staring hard at de Morales.

"Goodnight," he said to the other men, many of whom were squirming at the sudden tension.

As he walked away, Carlos upbraided himself for talking too much, for exposing too much of his heart to fools. Yet at the same time he was seething with a quiet rage at the mocking tone de Morales had used when he said, "There will never be a God Carlos."

Those insulting words were still ringing in his ears when Carlos woke up in a dark spot under the overhang of the quarterdeck, where he usually slept. His heart was suppurating hate as if infected by an abscess.

CHAPTER 6

od Carlos: that was the mocking nickname the crew, at the instigation of de Morales, began to secretly call Carlos behind his back. But the *Santa Inez* was a small ship alone on a big sea, and it was easy to misread malice, malignity even, in every gesture and sidelong look.

One morning as he was strolling near the mainmast where some men were gathered talking, he heard the name God Carlos muttered in a contemptuous tone for the first time. When the men saw him, they immediately fell quiet and feigned an indifferent innocence.

Carlos walked past them, headed for his customary spot on the vessel near the bow, and though he nodded at every man with whom he made eye contact, he had to struggle to keep his face expressionless as if he'd heard nothing.

The dolphins were playing on either side of the bow as the ship cut through the small furrowed waves with a tearing sound. Carlos was in a wretched mood and throbbing with such hate that though he tried to hide what he felt, the rage shadowed his every look and gesture. On a small ship at sea there was no way to withdraw with dignity, to remove himself from the taunts and sly looks. Everywhere Carlos went he was conscious that sailors might be whispering about him, and even if they were not, the very thought that they might be was enough to make him enraged.

He particularly hated using the *jardines*—the seats hung over the fore and aft rails for the men to relieve themselves. He refused to sit on these during the daylight while other men were present on deck unless he could not help it. Instead, he would wait until darkness had fallen and only a skeleton crew was on watch. Then he would use the most forward jardine where he would be out of sight to anyone on the quarterdeck and barely visible to the lookout in the crow's nest.

For the next few days, he was morose and quiet and avoided any gathering of men. He kept away from everyone with such persistence that hardly anyone sought him out for companionship and lighthearted talk. Old Hernandez was the only one who would regularly drift to where he was standing and exchange a few words with him. The boy Pedro would also occasionally wave from across the deck, and one Sunday morning he sat nearby on the bow of the ship and talked idly about the life he had lived in the foothills of the Pyrénées.

Carlos listened without a change of expression, making no remark in return no matter what the boy said. It was only because he did not wish to offend that Pedro did not simply get up and leave in the face of this impassive treatment. Instead, he stayed sitting where he was and told his story bravely as though Carlos was listening intently to every word. When he was done, the boy got up and said goodbye and ambled away.

The hideous nickname of God Carlos soon reached the ears of de la Serena and made him worry. He had once been young and hot-blooded himself, and understanding the nature of seamen well, he feared what would happen next.

But he said nothing to Carlos. And though on an impulse, he had summoned de Morales to his cabin for a chastising talk, he changed his mind at the last minute and said nothing about the conflict. Boys would be boys, and men would be men, and de la Serena only hoped that neither man would push the other too far.

The *Santa Inez* had been at sea now for twenty-one days, scudding to the trade winds with a bone in her teeth. Every day had been mild and glorious, with fleecy white clouds sprinkled throughout a clear blue sky. The wind blew out of the northeast at a steady fifteen knots, making perfect sailing weather. Rolling gently to a quartering wind, the *Santa Inez* made a susurration of contentment.

The fresh sparkling days that had followed one another in unvarying succession made the men eager to awaken in the mornings and gaze upon the splendors of the ocean. No rain fell for a whole week, and then for several afternoons came a brief shower that rinsed the salt off the men and the ship and left everyone feeling refreshed. The nights were cool, and the constellations spangled overhead with a breathtaking clarity.

It was all that a mariner could ask for, and de la Serena in his morning and evening prayers made a point of thanking God for the gentleness He had shown the ship.

One night Carlos was on the midnight watch, standing beside the compass on the quarterdeck. Around him the ship slumbered, with shadowy humps of men scattered over the deck, asleep. The wind had slackened, and the *Santa Inez* was barely making steerage speed.

De la Serena stepped onto the quarterdeck, cast a glance at the night sky, looking for the North Star. Then he recognized Carlos.

"Ahh, Carlos," he greeted, "is all well with the ship?"

"All is well, señor," Carlos said mechanically.

De la Serena stared hard at the sky and shook his head. "Beautiful, beautiful," he said in a husky whisper. "What a pity there is no God."

Carlos was so shocked that he could only sputter, "Señor?"

"Oh, it is a secret, naturally. Only the pope knows. And, of course, I know. There is no God."

"But señor," Carlos protested, waving at the vast,

star-sprinkled heaven, "then who made all this?"

"No one. It has always been here. It is we who are new."

"I do not understand," Carlos mumbled. "How can you pray every day if you do not believe in God."

"I do it to comfort my crew. But no one is listening to our prayers. Because there is no one up there," and he jabbed a finger at the sky.

Carlos fell silent. He was not prepared to say that there was no God. That his own captain should say this to him was so unexpected that it left him speechless. He did not waste his time thinking about abstract things. Moreover, all around him were the mariner's principal treasures—a calm sea and a clear sky—and they could not have always been there. He stared into the dark sea and felt uncomfortable.

Finally, as if he had just awakened, he said in a small helpless voice, "But, señor, your prayers are so convincing!"

"It is because of all my practice," de la Serena sighed. "A rich man must constantly pray before others. It is expected of him. If he is poor, no one expects him to perform in public as though he were a bishop. But let him be rich, and he is forced to become a spectacle. If you are a religious man, pray that you never become rich."

None of this did Carlos understand. He did not understand irony, so it did not occur to him that perhaps de la Serena did not exactly mean what he had just said. What troubled him most was why the older man was telling him these perplexing things.

"So, if someone calls you God Carlos, it is not a bad thing. You might as well be God, since there is no other."

Carlos frowned and turned away in the darkness so the older man could not see his displeasure. Now it was clear to him why de la Serena was bringing up such a strange topic. He had gotten wind of Carlos's nickname, and he was trying to make light of it.

"That is why I need a new world, so I can name part of it after me. When I die, I die forever. No one will even know that I was ever here. That fraud, that bumbler, Amerigo Vespucci, will be remembered by the generations to come because his name has been given to a continent. I knew the man. He does not deserve to have even a sandbar named after him. Yet in a planisphere that came out a few years ago, two continents—two, I say, not one—were named for him. Does that sound like the fairness one would expect in a world created by a god?"

Carlos did not know what to say, so he said nothing, but pretended to be engrossed in reading the compass by the dim light of the cresset. He rapped on the open hatch to attract the helmsman's attention.

"Helmsman," he barked louder than he meant to, "steer five degrees to starboard."

"She has no steerage way," the helmsman grumbled. "The wind is too light."

"It will pick up with daylight," Carlos said. "Just hold the course as steady as you can."

De la Serena, meanwhile, was leaning over the rail of the quarterdeck and staring at the dark, calm sea that caressed the rounded hull of the ship.

After a long silence, Carlos stirred and muttered, "I do not deserve this trouble. I am a peaceful man."

"It is the sea that vexes men's souls and leaves them hating each other," de la Serena murmured sympathetically.

Carlos walked over to the ampolleta, whose sand had almost run out, and stared intensely. He inverted the hourglass just as the final grains of sand tumbled out of one side, while de la Serena silently watched.

Around them could be heard the gurgling sounds of a wooden ship adrift in a calm night sea. With every slight correction of the rudder came the loud groan of wood against wood. The sails were flapping listlessly in the windless sea, and the cobwebby rigging of the ship was heavy with glittering stars.

The men had nothing more to say to each other. De la Serena said, "It is a bright night, though there is no moon."

"Yes," Carlos mumbled. "It is bright."

"Goodnight, then," de la Serena said, heading down the hatch for his private quarters.

"Goodnight, señor," Carlos replied, flicking his gaze over the sails of the ship.

* * *

The next day, with the *Santa Inez* becalmed in an unusual stillness for this latitude, many of the crew spontaneously decided to swim. Several dove overboard and frolicked beside the drifting ship while one man climbed the crow's nest to look out for sharks. Most of the men owned only the clothes on their backs, so they swam naked, some even taking advantage of the unnatural calm to wash the only pair of pantaloons and linen shirt they owned.

Carlos was off the morning watch, having been on duty from three a.m. to five, but his natural modesty inclined him not to swim. He thought that later on, if there was still no wind after darkness had fallen, he would wash his only clothes. In the meantime, he wanted to find a place on deck where he could snatch a brief nap.

He was amidships, passing a group of frolicking naked men when de Morales, who was fully clothed and had not been swimming, jeered, "Will God Carlos not go for a swim among humans?"

Some of the men laughed. Others fell eerily silent, sensing the spore of menace in the moment, that what had been spoken was not a harmless taunt, but carried a deadlier threat. It was inconceivable that such poisonous words would not be sharply answered.

Carlos stopped and slowly turned to face his antagonist. Inside him, an insurmountable rage was building, but he struggled hard to hide his true feelings.

"Do not let me hear you call me that name, señor," he said icily. "I do not like it."

De Morales would not let it go. He snickered. "What will you do to me, God Carlos, strike me dead?"

Words alone were an insufficient answer to such public scorn, and Carlos immediately knew that. He slapped de Morales hard on the left cheek with his open hand, snapping the other's head violently back.

That was also unanswerable with words. De Morales pulled out his dagger, bellowed a roar of anger, and slashed wildly at Carlos.

Carlos drew his own knife, shied out of reach, and waited for his opportunity while the other flailed away, wielding his dagger like a man deranged.

One savage stroke hissed wide, and for a blink de Morales was awkwardly twisted by the momentum of his own mad swing, his side bared open and unprotected.

Seizing de Morales by the shoulder and clasping him close, Carlos lunged like a cobra and drove the knife deep into the side of the other man's chest. The dagger sank into flesh like it was warm pudding. For a brief moment, the two men seemed locked in a deadly mating dance, Carlos gripping the knife with one hand while steadying de Morales to receive the full thrust of the blade with the other.

His eyes bursting open with shock and disbelief, de Morales slumped grudgingly, like a coyly consenting lover, into the arms of his killer, who still clutched the penetrating blade buried down to the hilt.

"Holy Mother of God! I can't breathe!" he gasped. Blood spewed in dark, brocade-rich clumps from his mouth.

Then he fell to the deck, dead.

There was an accounting afterward of the events and words that led to this woeful incident, and an informal court of inquiry was convened and presided over by de la Serena to find out what exactly had happened between the two men to have brought matters to such a tragic end. Men on both sides testified, and although Carlos had few supporters, he had provocation and taunting to explain his behavior.

De la Serena pieced together a patchwork version of what had happened and ruled the homicide justified as self-defense. Some of de Morales's friends and shipmates were unhappy with this conclusion, especially since Carlos admitted striking the first blow. But under the circumstances, de la Serena said ruefully, a man could have given no other reply without a severe loss of face. And though some of the men grumbled, in their hearts they knew the captain was right.

After the inquiry, there was a funeral. The body of the dead man was wrapped in a piece of sailcloth and weighted down with a few stone cannonballs taken from the four Lombard cannons mounted in carriages on the deck.

A day after the fight, on a clear and windy morning, a brief funeral service was held aboard the *Santa Inez*. De la Serena read from the 23rd Psalm, all the crew attended, and after the reading, the body was ceremoniously hurled into the sea.

The body struck the calm surface with a startling splash, loud and vulgar like ejected excrement. It rolled and burrowed into the bottomless blue as the ship ghosted away in a light morning breeze. A moment later no eye could tell where it had fallen, the crinkled surface of the ocean being so vast and changeless all around the creeping vessel.

No one knew where de Morales had come from or where his family was, and since he had been unable to write, the dead man had left no identifying documents behind. It was as if he had never lived.

Carlos was branded a murderer by some of his shipmates. Others thought his action justified but excessive. De la Serena announced at the end of the inquiry that his official ruling would be entered into the log and become part of the history of the *Santa Inez* and this voyage.

She had been at sea now for twenty-eight days.

CHAPTER 7

A *neke?"* Why?

That was what Orocobix, with anguish in his voice, asked the *zemi* propped up against the trunk of a nearby seagrape tree.

His Uncle Brayou was dying alone somewhere in the woods, and Orocobix was pleading to the zemi for mercy. But the zemi was not answering, even though it had answered others in the past.

For example, his mother swore that one evening when her heart was torn with trouble and she begged the zemi for comfort, it had replied with soothing words. No one else had heard them, however, for she was alone at the time. But he believed his mother. And he was disappointed that the zemi would not now talk to him. Surely, being a god, the zemi should understand how deeply he was troubled. But it was being hardhearted and saying nothing.

It was March 29, 1520, a Thursday. But Orocobix, who was an Arawak Indian, knew neither the day nor the year, for he could not write and had no calendar.

However, he knew that it was still the rainy season and the time of the year when the wind sometimes blows fiercely from the north and for several days the sea is torn by huge white waves. He also knew that it was not the season to worry about *huraca'ns*—hurricanes—which during the warm months would sometimes ravage the island with a cataclysmic wind and rain, uprooting enormous trees and changing the shapes of rivers.

He poignantly knew that it was time for his Uncle Brayou, who had grown old and frail, to travel to the land where sky-dwelling gods walked on clouds and where the sky was always blue and everywhere was dancing and feasting.

Yet his Uncle Brayou had a dark fear in his heart about dying. He would not admit it, but Orocobix knew and had asked the zemi to help.

And the zemi did nothing and said nothing.

Orocobix looked out to sea as if for an answer, but saw only the distant reef lined by a glistening lace of shimmering surf. He stared at the sky, which was bright and tinged with a brilliant blue so thick that the very air seemed palpable and crystalline like spring water, and the sky had no answer.

He was standing on the shore of what Columbus had called Santa Gloria Bay, now St. Ann's Bay, on an island the Indians knew variously as Yamaca or Xamaca or Hamaica, but whose name has come down to us as Jamaica.

What the word originally meant no one knows today, although the tourist brochures and guidebooks claim its meaning was "land of wood and water."

Others have guessed that it meant "land of springs." Still others say it meant "land of cotton." But whatever the origin of its name, Xamaca was the only island in the Indies that Columbus called "the fairest that eyes have beheld."

Orocobix was a brown man of twenty-five, well-proportioned, with dark straight hair hanging down the back of his neck. His forehead, thick and sloping like a slab of upraised bone, was the most distinctive feature of his face.

It was a look the Arawaks created by tying boards to the foreheads of their newborns. Why they did this is inexplicable today, but if intended for aesthetics this odd custom had at least the practical effect of making the Arawak forehead so tough that in combat clubs and swords often shattered against it.

Curling out of the sand like the bony claws of a sea monster were the rotting remains of two wrecked caravels, *Capitana* and *Santiago*, which Admiral Columbus had abandoned seventeen years earlier in Santa Gloria Bay on his fourth and last voyage to the Indies when shipworms had made the vessels unseaworthy.

It was in this very spot that the gods from the sky had worked a great miracle, causing a serpent to devour the moon and spit it out again only after the Arawaks had publicly repented for being inhospitable to the marooned foreigners and vowed to do better.

Orocobix did not know it now, and would never know it, but the miracle Columbus had performed for the Arawaks had come not from the Spanish god, but from a German book, the *Ephemerdies* of Regiomontanus, which forecast a total eclipse of the moon on February 29, 1504.

When the Indians would not feed the gluttonous appetite of his marooned crew—one Spaniard ate as much in a day as an Arawak did in a week—Columbus warned the *caciques* of the surrounding tribes that the Spanish god would devour the moon as a warning of the pestilence and famine they would be punished with for mistreating the shipwrecked Spaniards. And then the moon was devoured, just as the god from the sky had predicted, causing widespread panic, consternation, and wailing repentance among the Indians.

All this magic happened when Orocobix was a boy of eight. Even then he was a devout believer in the zemi and slept with it at his side. All his life he had believed with heart and soul.

The zemi, representing the great god Yocahuna, was now resting against the trunk of a seagrape tree, looking inscrutable. It was made of dark wood carved in the image of a bird that had the feet of a man, a prominent beak permanently impregnated with a sidelong painted grin, and two arms jutting from its side like wings except that they were tipped by what looked suspiciously like fingers. In truth, the effigy was hideous, and liking it—to say nothing of idolizing it—took a zealot's devoutness.

On the day that Orocobix stood on the seashore,

the Arawaks had already been in Jamaica for an un-known period of time, perhaps hundreds, even thou-sands of years. Although Orocobix did not know the origins of his people but believed they had always lived in Jamaica, their roots actually extended to the Orinoco River and Delta Amacuro.

The Taíno people to whom the island Arawaks and Orocobix belonged had puddle-jumped their way up the Lesser Antilles over the past centuries, driving ahead of them an even more primitive Stone Age peo-ple known as the Siboneys. Using as stepping stones the islands of the archipelago, the Arawaks moved into the Greater Antilles displacing the slow-witted Siboneys from Puerto Rico, Hispaniola, Cuba, and Ja-maica. What happened to the people they dislodged, no one knows, and on this day in 1520 when Orocobix stood on the shore, the Siboneys were nearly extinct.

Now the same implacable fate was threatening the Arawak. Already they had been driven from the Lesser Antilles by the fierce Carib Indians, a savage, warlike people who ate their male Arawak captives and bred their females. His village had been struck by these murderous raiders many times and several Ar-awak children taken to be caponized—their testicles removed—making them soft and fat for the roasting spit. The raiders were wicked *canaballi*, cannibals, and just thinking about them made Orocobix shudder.

Orocobix was naked. But he was not self-conscious

about his nakedness, for he had never worn clothes. His body was painted with black, white, and red dyes as adornments to advertise his youth and manhood, and his right nostril was pierced with a small delicate ornament made from an alloy of gold and copper the Indians called *guanin*. He did not know it, but the dyes protected his skin against the pitiless sun like a lotion.

He stood on the shore of the land he belonged to and loved deeply as his home and asked his god again, "Aneke?" Why?

Why would the zemi not help Uncle Brayou who lay dying alone in his hammock somewhere in the bush?

If Brayou had been a cacique, his counselors would have sent his soul peacefully to *coyaba*—Arawak heaven—by quietly strangling him one night as he slept.

But Brayou was an ordinary man whose time had come. And in spite of all the desperate pleas of Orocobix, the zemi said nothing and made no move to help.

"*Naboria daca*," Orocobix said humbly. I am your servant. Help me, please.

Orocobix gently picked up the zemi and headed toward the sloping grasslands fringing the foothills. He was following a footpath marked out over the years by Arawaks going back and forth between the village at the foot of the mountains and the sea. As Orocobix walked he was careful not to bump the zemi against any overhanging bush, but sheltered his god protectively under one of his arms.

Following the footpath, he entered the woodland and made his way into the dense foliage until he came to a clearing where he found Uncle Brayou dozing on his hammock slung between two jagua trees.

The elders had brought his uncle here following a long-established Arawak custom of taking the dying with their hammocks to a place where they could be left to die alone in dignity. It was what was done when an Indian was old or sick beyond hope. On the ground next to the hammock the elders had thoughtfully left some cassava bread and a gourd of water.

Orocobix, on seeing that his uncle was asleep, tried to sneak away without disturbing him, but the old man opened his eyes and cried, "Orocobix, am I in coyaba?"

Orocobix drew close to the hammock and whispered to his uncle, as Arawaks do in the presence of death, "No, Uncle."

The old man began shaking, his body raging with a fever. Orocobix touched him gently on the arms and whispered, "I have prayed to the zemi for you. But so far, he has not answered me."

Uncle Brayou laughed loudly. "He is wood. You expect an answer from wood? Wood has no tongue to speak."

"Uncle!" Orocobix scolded, making a shushing motion with his hands. "The zemi will hear your blasphemy and be offended."

Uncle Brayou sagged into the hammock and

laughed so hard that he began coughing. Orocobix stroked him gently on the back.

When he recovered, Uncle Brayou gasped, "Wood has no feelings. Oh, Orocobix, you are such a child."

"One day, Uncle, you will see that I was right and you were wrong. Then you will appreciate the zemi for its protection."

Uncle Brayou coughed and spat an ugly chunk of green spittle, which nearly hit the zemi straight on the beak.

It was an old argument that had raged between them since Orocobix was a child. Even on his death-bed, Uncle remained stubborn and would not be moved.

Uncle Brayou was one of the bravest and strongest of his generation. One time when the village was under attack, Uncle Brayou killed three of the raiders by himself, using a spear taken from a Carib warrior. He had the heart of a fighter, but he was also a woeful unbeliever. And even though age and disease had struck him down and he had been taken out into the bush to die, he still would not recant his disbeliefs. The Arawak zemis were not gods but statues made of wood or stone. Yocahuna did not exist. Others may have thought such terrible things, but Uncle Brayou spoke them openly to all who would listen.

Orocobix gathered up the zemi carefully in his arms, said goodbye to his uncle, and headed toward the village.

"Orocobix," his uncle was shrieking in a surprisingly strong voice, "you might as well pray to my hammock! If that wood is God, so's my hammock."

Orocobix did not answer the taunt, for any reply would only goad Uncle to harsher blasphemies. What he had already said was enough to bar him from entering coyaba.

The young Indian walked doggedly through the thicket, waving to his uncle without looking back and pretended not to hear the sacrilegious words.

In his painted arms, he cradled the zemi gently as if he were carrying a newborn.

CHAPTER 8

Brayou passed sometime that night in the presence of no loved ones or even indifferent onlookers. The next morning, Orocobix found him curled up in his hammock like a man not asleep but dead.

It was time for weeping. Orocobix stood silently beside the hammock on which his dead uncle lay, and he wept. He touched his uncle on the arm and felt the chill and stiffness of death. The zemi said nothing about his sorrow and made no move to console him. So Orocobix just stood beside the hammock, with the sadness pouring out of him.

Brayou had been a big man when he was young, but age had shrunk him over the years. Now there were two uncles, the little naked one who was shriveled up dead on the hammock, and the big, strong one who lived on in Orocobix's mind.

A black bird perched on a nearby branch and sang a lighthearted song almost boisterously until Orocobix threw a stone and drove it away. Then he was sorry for he thought it might have been a sign sent by his uncle. From somewhere in the woods came the song again, and Orocobix felt consoled.

He did not know how old his uncle was. He did not know what had killed him. He did not know his uncle's birthday. He had no name for this day, but it was marked forever in his heart as a day of pain and grief. He would observe it in his memory, and it would never leave him, but without a calendar and with no writing, Orocobix would have no anniversary of his uncle's death and no way to remember to mourn it with the passing years. He would remember only that the uncle died at the end of the rainy season and before the coming of the hot weather that brought hurricanes.

Unlike the Spaniards, Arawaks like Orocobix felt the years flow past only in the rhythm of the seasons. The naming of days and months and the mechanical segmentation of time into repetitious and measured units was beyond them because they had no writing.

European Romanticists would later celebrate the West Indian Arawak as a man of nature and praise his unlettered ignorance as if it were a blessing. But illiteracy and naturalness are no blessings if all they do is make you easier prey for literate invaders. Over the next century the privileged sons of Europe would gather in brocaded drawing rooms to read asinine poetry extolling Arawaks as *noble savages*—all this while her armies of *conquistadors* and adventurers would be kept busy slaughtering these mythical innocents.

These ruminations and speculations, however, were beyond the grieving young Arawak. As he stood over the hammock on which the dead man lay curled up, Orocobix felt that he should go and inform the elders that Brayou had become a *goeiz*—a spirit—before he took the body to the burial cave, for it was his obligation to let them know. But his heart was still burning with anger that the elders had not strangled Brayou in his sleep as they would have a cacique.

He was thinking about what he should do when he heard the crackle of approaching footsteps. He darted behind a bush and crouched low and rummaged over the ground for anything he could use as a weapon in case the intruders were marauding Caribs. Finding a big stone half buried in the dirt among the tangled roots of a bush, he dug it out with his fingernails and clutched it in his right hand like a club while he kept his eyes riveted on the trail.

As the footfalls drew nearer, Orocobix tensed and held the stone ready. He was crouching behind the bush when he saw an old man limping along with the aid of a stick toward the hammock, glancing around like a frightened bird. He was naked and had a full head of graying hair, but he looked like no one else Orocobix had ever seen. He stooped over as if weighted down by a heavy load on his back, and his legs were as crooked and thin as drought-stricken bamboo. His entire body was covered by a fine pelt of thin hair. What was most curious about his features was that he was missing the thick forehead of the Arawak.

But it was the fear and furtiveness of the intruder

that Orocobix noticed first. He acted like a preyed-upon wild animal that sensed it was being stalked, and with almost every move he paused to gaze around him, his small eyes darting from bush to tree, his frame freezing against the foliage while he cocked his head, sniffed the air, and listened.

He saw the hammock, and his eyes flitted indifferently over the dead body and came to rest, burning with hunger, at the pieces of cassava bread that the elders had left for Brayou.

His eyes fixed on the cassava bread, he was making his way cautiously toward it when the sound of approaching footsteps thumped softly on the morning wind like a baby's heartbeat. The old man spun in his tracks, glanced longingly at the cassava bread before plunging into the thicket with surprising stealth and melting into the foliage. He had just disappeared when a group of elders emerged into the clearing, talking animatedly among themselves.

One of them was the shaman of the tribe, Guaniquo. He was in a bad mood, and when he noticed Orocobix, his face darkened with anger.

"Brayou is gone?" he asked abruptly, making a gesture of impatience with his right hand.

"He is gone, Guaniquo. He went sometime during the night."

"It is well that he is gone, Orocobix," said Guaroco, who everyone in the tribe said was the oldest and wisest of the elders.

"He went alone, with no one to watch him go," Orocobix said bitterly.

"And what would watching him have changed?" Guaniquo asked harshly. "Would you have caught his spirit and held it back so it could not fly away into the darkness?"

There was a long, strained silence while Orocobix carefully weighed his reply. He was tempted to speak some sharp words, but the combined presence of the elders momentarily cowed him and made him hold his temper. "When your own time comes, Guaniquo," he said carefully, "we will see how eager you are to take that journey."

"The time must come for all of us," one of the elders muttered. "There is no cause to fear."

"What is that doing here?" Guaniquo suddenly demanded to know, pointing at the zemi that Orocobix had placed against a nearby tree. "It is unclean for the zemi to be in a place of death."

"He goes where I go," Orocobix said defiantly. "If he were displeased, he would tell me so."

"Zemis do not talk to everyone," Guaroco said cautiously, flicking a deferential glance at the shaman, who was known to be very jealous of anyone else's claim to be able to talk to the gods.

"It is a way of the young," Guaniquo, the shaman, spat. "They would claim privileges without fasting, without sacrifice, without a knowledge of the gods. It is the times. That is why the gods from the sky have come among us. That is why many of them are so cruel to our people."

Orocobix almost laughed out loud, which would have been sacrilegious with Uncle Brayou lying dead nearby, but again he held himself in check.

"I am not to be blamed for the movement of gods, Guaniquo," he said. "Gods can do as they please."

Guaroco interposed with the weight of his years. "It is enough," he said. "Brayou must be taken to the place where all eventually go."

Orocobix nodded, asked Guaroco if he would carry the zemi for him, then gathered his dead uncle in his arms, and set out heavily toward the burial cave. His uncle was light but burdensome because his limbs had stiffened and his flesh had grown cold. And even though the elders offered to help him, Orocobix said no, and continued carrying his uncle on the trail that led to the burial place.

Every now and again, especially after the trail had wound up a little slope, he would set his uncle's body gently on the ground and take a brief rest.

Everywhere around them was a surrounding loveliness, a benignity of climate, and a land softly rising in undulations of flowering bushes and trees. The day was mild and stirred by a soft breeze. Being naked, Orocobix reacted to climactic conditions like an animal, with an innate sense of comfort and discomfort. He did not know what temperature meant or how it would be measured more than a hundred years later by the German physicist Gabriel Daniel Fahrenheit. He only knew that on this day he was hot from the burden of carrying his dead uncle, but when he could sit in the shade and rest, he felt cool. The year-round sameness of the island's climate made this day seem no different from the rest.

Again the elders offered to help him with the load, but he politely refused. One elder complained that it was the custom for several hands to bear a dead man to the burial cave, but when Orocobix insisted that he could do it alone, none of the old men argued with him.

Occasionally, someone heading for the seacoast would come tramping down the trail, encounter the funeral procession, and look to see who had died. All the passersby had known Brayou. In the Arawak village lived about seven hundred souls, and everyone knew everyone else, if not deeply, then at least by name and kinship. Some of the passersby touched the dead body with respect and reverence as if to say goodbye. Others made a clucking sound with their tongues in quiet lamentation and averted their eyes as if not to see an unclean sight.

In death, every part of Brayou, as he had been in life, was physically revealed to the sky, the sun, the wind, and to every passing eye. He had lived his entire life naked, and in death he was also naked, giving him the appearance of a defenseless creature that had crawled out of its protective shell. Every runic scar that the adventures of a long life had engraved on his flesh stood out in stark relief like an embossed hieroglyphic.

A few passersby were moved by the sight of the dead man, and one or two women continued down the trail emitting a faint ululation of mourning. Uncle had died an old man, and the last years of his life had found him crotchety and blunt. There would be a feast to honor his death, but other than his immediate family, few in the tribe would truly mourn his loss.

With frequent stops to rest, Orocobix, flanked by the solemn clutch of elders, trudged up the hillside and eventually came to the burial cave.

Inside, he placed Brayou's body atop a pile of old bones. Strewn throughout the dimness of the cave were skulls of Arawaks, young and old, all baring the humorless grin of the ancient dead. To some skulls a tuft of dark hair clung like a stubborn moss. Rib cages, emptied of lungs and viscera decades ago, curled symmetrical bones around the empty abdominal cavity like a partly clenched fist. Scattered all over the damp floor of the cave were elongated femurs, tibia shadowed by fibula, all etching in bone the shape of some long-dead Arawak. Painted on the walls of the cave, curious shapes and geometric figures bore mute testimony to an unknown mourner's stifled grief. Every breath Orocobix and the elders drew in that cave tasted ripe with decay like the smell of a rotting tooth.

Orocobix had to lay Uncle down on top of old,

dislodged bones, as there was no room left in the cave for a body to lie by itself. He arranged the body as comfortably as he could.

"We need another burying place," old Guaroco muttered sympathetically. "There's almost no room left for me."

"It is the young today who are too lazy to seek one," Guaniquo said crossly.

Guaniquo performed the ceremony of the dead, scattering some dust over the dead man and muttering incantations known only to him because of their secret powers. Orocobix stood with his head bowed, remembering his uncle as a younger man, and half listening to the shaman. At the mouth of the cave stood the remaining elders, their heads hanging as a sign of respect.

Then everyone filed out of the cave and into the bright sunlight where the air smelled of blossoming trees and flowering plants and an enormous flock of parrots fluttered overhead in the breeze like a skein of green and blue tapestry, dragging behind them a gliding shadow.

No one spoke, but it was clear from the long sighs of the elders that they were all glad to be away from the place of death. They trooped down the footpath toward the village, each man keeping his thoughts to himself.

Orocobix said, like a man thinking aloud, "I wonder if Brayou will like *guabasa*."

Guaroco chuckled. "He had better grow to like it," the old man said. "It is all that spirits eat."

"I do not know if I would like having nothing but that to eat," one of the elders said contemplatively. "I'd rather stay here and eat fish and turtle."

A titter of amusement arose from the old men, and everyone felt normal again and relieved to be out in the sunlight and alive in the breeze on this day, March 30, in the year of our Lord Yochuna, 1520.

That night a feast was held. The dead man's clan built a bonfire and there was singing and dancing and reminiscing about Brayou.

The older generation remembered Brayou mainly for his sacrilegious opinions about zemis, but a few also recalled the night when the canaballi had attacked the village, and Brayou had killed three of them with their own spears, sending the others fleeing into the night. He'd had no sons or daughters of his own, even though he had lain with many women. His *moin*—his blood—was bad, the women said, and that was why he had no children.

But now that Brayou was gone, the people gathered at the feast spoke about him the way people everywhere speak of the recently dead, with affection and forgiveness. Some of the women wept quietly, more for themselves than for Brayou. Everyone had a favorite memory to tell, and all listened respectfully to the stories.

The crackling fire chewed a ragged chunk out of the tropical night and bathed everyone in a shimmering red and yellow hue. Children wandered among the adults looking stupefied. Occasionally, someone would dance to unheard rhythms, and someone would laugh out loud, and everywhere in the background came the drizzle of convivial banter. *Alcos*—the small, barkless dogs that Arawaks kept as pets and an emergency food supply—roamed everywhere throughout the gathered throng, making a ratlike squeaky sound of excitement and playing friskily with the children.

So it was a celebration of a long life, and it was also a feast tinged with sadness as the fate of Brayou reminded people of the journey that also lay ahead for them and their loved ones.

The shaman told stories of wonder and magic during a lull in the feasting, and everyone respectfully listened to tales about the zemis and the gods and coyaba. He spoke particularly about the gods that now roamed among them, the gods from the sky whose coming had long been prophesied and who now dwelled not so far away in a settlement they had recently built.

Only a few of the assembled men and women had ever actually seen these gods, and some would not speak of them because of shame. Among them was a young woman who had gone to the river and encountered three of the gods. She had never admitted it to anyone, for then she would have to tell the shameful

story of what the gods had done to her, one after another, and how she had been torn open and left on the
riverbank bleeding.

She had been confused and shamed to have been
so ill-used by the gods and felt that she must have
done something wrong to cause their displeasure. She
was an unmarried girl, barely sixteen, and she wor-
ried that if the village knew about what they had done
to her, no one would take her as a wife.

Among the assemblage were some young men
who had also witnessed the cruelty of the gods. One
of them had seen with his own eyes one of the gods
take a thunder stick and strike down an Arawak from
another village and then laugh joyfully about it. He
had reported what he had seen to the cacique—the
hereditary ruler of the tribe—and had been told to say
nothing to anyone else lest his story awake terror in
the hearts of the people.

The shaman had heard some of the stories, but he
did not believe them. He thought that the gods were
good, but being gods, they were beyond understanding. One must simply accept what the gods do and
pray that they will be merciful.

This was the orthodoxy that the shaman preached,
speaking in the superior tone of one who knew. He
had to know, for if he did not know, what good was
he as a shaman? So when he spoke about the gods, his
voice was like a papal encyclical, and no one could
doubt him.

As for Orocobix, his heart was the heaviest among the people at the feast, for he had loved his uncle. Brayou had raised him after Orocobix's parents had both been killed in a hurricane. Beside him at the feast sat old Yguana, Brayou's last surviving sister, but her head was filled with the dizziness that came from smoking leaves of *cohiba*—the tobacco plant—and other than smiling at the revelers and nodding dumbly to the occasional expression of mourning, she did not care.

The shaman told how the original two Arawaks had lived with the sun in a cave watched over by a guardian. But one day their guardian became careless and the sun escaped. Left in the darkness, the two Arawaks were forced to exit the cave and follow the light of the sun until they came to Xamaca. Here they made their home and lived in peace and contentment until the coming of the canaballi—the devourer of children. It was their punishment for leaving the cave that the canaballi had been sent to torment them.

As the shaman told his story, which everyone except for very small children had heard many times before, the cacique of the tribe—a young man by the name of Datijao—came and sat near Orocobix, paying a great honor to the memory of Brayou.

The shaman nodded respectfully to the cacique, and continued his story, with the revelers drawn in a tight circle around the blazing fire, listening intently as the flames ate up the night and blotted out the stars and exuded such a sapping heat that heads, old and young, began to nod.

There was a beginning, murmured the shaman, and the older people muttered sleepy assents. Indeed, life had had a beginning just as it had an ending.

Orocobix listened, though he knew the recital by heart having heard it a countless number of times before. Deep within him he had a hunger to believe. And he did believe. He said it so intensely to himself that he shivered as though stricken by a sudden chill. The shaman noticed with pleasure, thinking that it was his telling of the story that had made Orocobix spasm.

CHAPTER 9

Aboard a sailing ship at sea, seamen often smell land long before they even glimpse it. At four a.m. one morning, Carlos was on the dog watch when he caught the aromatic whiff of blossoms and spices wafting from a distant land. For a moment, he felt the exhilaration of landfall that strikes every sailor at the end of a long voyage, and in his delight, he paced the poop deck restlessly, unable to contain his excitement. He looked around the deck of the dark ship for someone to talk to about what he had smelled.

There was a watch forward, but he was an Azorean and had been a friend of de Morales. Carlos did not trust him and was wary whenever he came near. There was the helmsman below deck, but he was holed up in the cramped steerage and had to keep his mind focused on the handling of the ship. Moreover, he too had been a *compadre* of the slain man and Carlos was not sure whose side he took in the dispute.

The *Santa Inez* had been at sea now for thirty straight days, and she was showing signs of wear. Her pumps had to be manned constantly to keep her afloat. *Teredos*—shipworms—were eating her bottom planking. She was also badly in need of careening which would involve beaching her and then scraping and re-caulking her hull with oakum and pitch. Seawater had seeped into her bilge and she was beginning to wallow. Already the helmsman could feel the sluggishness in her steering.

It had been an uneasy voyage for Carlos since he'd killed de Morales. He trusted no one. Always a loner, he kept even more stubbornly to himself, and when anyone drew too near him, he would openly slide his hand toward the dagger in his waist. If he was standing at the railing and anyone approached him, he would immediately step back with a glowering look of warning at the intruder to draw no closer.

So he was especially glad for the smell of land in the darkness ahead of the ship. Land meant space between him and other men. It meant he could withdraw and brood when he was in a bad mood. He could be truly alone. Aboard ship, although he could sit by himself in the bow, someone else was always near at hand and within earshot.

Old Hernandez was the only other person he partly trusted—aside from the boy Pedro, who sometimes trailed after him when they were both off duty. To the rest of the crew, he was an outcast they shunned.

Carlos did not think this was such a bad thing. It meant that none of them would come near enough to him under the guise of friendliness to bump him overboard or to stab him when he wasn't looking.

He ate his meals forward squatting on the deck by

himself and never in company. It was the one time of
the day when a man was most vulnerable, his attention
focused on filling his belly and not on the nearby eater
who might be an assassin. Once, as he was squatting
on the deck eating bread and cheese, a crewman came
and sat within a pike length of him and Carlos stared
hard at the man until he got up and sauntered away as
if indifferent. Perhaps the man meant no harm. But at
sea a man who had killed another in a fight could not
be too cautious.

Carlos felt particularly vulnerable at night. He
knew from experience that darkness at sea was a
cloak for much wickedness. Yet in the normal rota-
tion of the crew he had his share of midnight watches.
Sometimes, this would mean he was in charge of su-
pervising the turning of the ampolleta. On a pious
ship this ritual would be accompanied by a chant either made up by the seaman who turned the glass or
one that was commonly known to the fraternity of
sailors. On the *Santa Inez* only an Andalusian grommet named Alonzo who liked to sing observed this
tradition. Usually he would chant an impromptu
ditty such as this one, in a shrill voice loud enough
to be heard by all but not likely to awaken the deep
sleepers:

> *The third hour passeth*
> *All is well on God's good ship.*
> *Lookouts be sharp and vigilant*

For we sail alone on a merciless sea.
May almighty God bless our voyage.

On this particular night, the *Santa Inez* was so far south that she was nosing her way through untrafficked waters. She did not fear collision at sea. At best, with a following wind, she was capable of seven knots, hardly a breakneck pace that would shatter her if she hit another ship. And given the direction of the wind, which blew off her quarter or off her beam, she was hardly likely to encounter another vessel going in the opposite direction with whom she might collide. What a ship in her circumstances risked was a mid-ocean encounter with a whale or an uncharted island. But by far the greatest danger was the possibility of a sudden squall with high winds and heavy seas that would require reefing the sails or temporarily changing course.

So the nightwatch required a sailor to be alert. But a veteran seaman like Carlos also found the night a relaxing time when a man could be at peace and lose himself in thought. He was trying to imagine what the land he could smell so keenly must look like in the sunshine when a hatch opened and de la Serena clambered onto the deck. Carlos waited for the older man's eyes to become accustomed to the dark sea before he called out to him.

"Land, señor!" Carlos said, his voice edged with excitement.

"Where? Do you see a light?" De la Serena peered anxiously down the deck.

"No light, señor. But I smell land." And as if to demonstrate, Carlos drew a loud breath, his nose held high, and acted as if the scents were enough to make him feel intoxicated.

"I don't smell anything," de la Serena replied sadly, sounding disappointed.

Carlos inhaled with an exaggerated loudness. "Oh," he said confidently, "it is land—beyond question."

"If it is land, it should be Hispaniola."

"Not Jamaica?"

"It is the way of the tradewinds," de la Serena muttered. "They take us farther east than we would wish. Our first landfall should be the island the Admiral called Hispaniola."

"But we will not stop there, señor?"

"No," de la Serena said crisply. "We steer straight for Jamaica, which is to the southwest."

"The ship is badly in need of careening," Carlos mumbled.

"I know what she needs," de la Serena snapped back. "She'll find it in Jamaica."

With that, de la Serena went forward to the bow where the Azorean seaman stood lookout, and peered into the dark night everywhere around the surging ship. He asked the Azorean if he thought landfall was ahead, but the man said he'd seen nothing. He asked him if he smelled anything, and the Azorean mumbled that he had always had a bad nose.

Telling the man gruffly to keep awake and alert, de la Serena walked back to the poop deck where Carlos stood watch.

"The forward watch says he sees and smells nothing," de la Serena said.

"Señor," Carlos responded firmly, "we will see land at the first light."

Still disbelieving, de la Serena moved to the starboard side of the ship and peered down the cambered deck for the sight of land. Then he did the same from the port side. Carlos watched him with amusement.

After standing at the port railing for five minutes, seeing and hearing nothing, de la Serena sighed like a lovelorn suitor, said goodnight, and went down below.

Left alone on the poop deck, Carlos inverted the ampolleta and returned to his reverie.

A sailing ship on the night sea is a magical thing. She creaks and groans like an old woman, and the wind in her sail is like a lover's whisper. The whole vessel moves with a sinuousness, every gentle lunge accompanied by a gurgling lullaby of wind and water.

The *Santa Inez* carried no running lights. A candle flickered in the cabin occupied by de la Serena, but its illumination was a pinpoint. On the poop deck where the compass was mounted, a blazing cresset threw off a jittery glow that allowed the watch to keep an eye

on the ship's heading and to turn the ampolleta. Voy-
aging on an ocean now as dark and mysterious as any
body of water on earth, the *Santa Inez*, unlit and un-
seeable like a hulking whale, was lumbering fearlessly
through the night.

A different man would have been caught up in the
beauty and loveliness that embraced the ship, and
his mind would have turned to mystical thoughts.
But Carlos had too proud a heart for even the magic
of the moment to soften. He was reliving the fight
obsessively—savoring the last desperate words of
his dead enemy and imagining, with a fierce exulta-
tion, the terror de Morales must have felt as the knife
plunged deep into his chest. Carlos was only twenty-
six and already he'd taken two lives.

How many men, other than hardened soldiers
whose job was to fight and kill, could say as much?
Indeed, there was something godlike about him, and
as he came to this conclusion, without knowing what
he was doing, his gait evolved as he strolled the poop
deck into the strut of a victorious rooster.

Once again he returned to his favorite dream of being a god, or of being seen to be godlike. This dream
was a reptile in a dark dungeon of his heart. And even
as he pored over it repeatedly, like a miser might fondle his cache of dirty money, he knew it was a terrible
fantasy but could not help himself for loving it.

He reflected that it was a good feature of creation
that men could not read the thoughts of others or tell

what was in another's heart, for then there would be
no peace. Enmity between men would be universal,
and they would long to kill one another. And then he
thought if the world were such a place, it would differ
little from the present one, and he was surprised at
himself for reaching such a lofty conclusion.

Truly, he had his philosophical moments; without
question, he was a thinker—not all the time, of course,
for he was basically a man of deeds, not thought—but
every now and again, he was capable of examining
creation and probing its deficiencies. He was quite
proud of himself.

So he walked the poop deck, kept an eye on the
compass lit by the cresset, and thought deeply about
the cracks in creation. But it was only a theoretical
probing and just for fun, he hastily added in case a
saint was listening. He had no complaints against the
earth. It was a good place that God had created. It
was a good ocean that the ship now sailed on—one of
God's masterpieces. And to make sure that the saint
understood, he recited the Pater Noster in Latin. He
did not understand its words, but many years ago, like
the other village boys, he had been forced to memorize
it. And he knew it was a good, sturdy prayer that God
and the angels liked to hear from the mouths of men.

When he had finished saying it, he felt refreshed
and cleansed. The unthinking, reflexive Catholic inside him imagined grace flooding into his soul and
healing it. But then, in the very next breath, his mind

turned to de Morales and the shameless effrontery of the man to give him a mocking nickname and then use it in the presence of others to his face, and the rage that sluiced through his loins made him wish he could kill his tormentor all over again.

So his thoughts ranged from imagined bigness to unacknowledged littleness, from rote piety to reptilian rage, and through it all he did not recognize the truth about himself: that he was a little man with a little soul, and a little, puffed up, unknowing heart that would make him as menacing to his new surroundings as a mutant, rogue bacillus.

The grayness in which the ship sailed was dissolving, signaling daybreak, and in the breeze Carlos could now strongly smell land.

Never mind that others could not smell it. He knew it was there, just ahead, skulking under the horizon. It was the land of a fresh new world, where he would be regarded as a god from the sky. He would be a good god. His worshippers would grow to love him.

Just as he was beginning to once again dream of his godhood, just as he was savoring it anew like a child returning to play with a favorite toy, just as the dawn light was slowly releasing the ship from its gray webbing, came the excited cry of the Azorean lookout in the bow of the ship: "Land, dead ahead!"

De la Serena bounded out of his cabin and sprang to the deck with surprising agility for an old man. Scattered around the deck, sleeping sailors began to stir and stood up to look. There on the horizon loomed a gray smudge against the skyline.

De la Serena turned to Carlos with a big grin. "Your nose, señor," he said effusively, "is a godlike instrument."

And then, realizing that he had misspoken, the older man made a gesture of self-reproof and drifted away among the celebrating crewmen. But Carlos was not angry. In fact, he was so pleased to have the ship owner talk to him with such respect that he mumbled, "Thank you, señor."

De la Serena, however, did not hear. Already he was craning toward the approaching, unseen land.

He sent the boy Pedro to fetch the charts from down below, and he sent another boy for the astrolabe—the primitive instrument mariners of his day used to navigate. He wanted to know, as close as possible, where the ship was, for he had the sailor's distrust of strange landforms. Around him, the crew, now eagerly awake, gathered, chattering with energy and goodwill.

On his orders, the *Santa Inez* hove to and slowly drifted to a near standstill. Ahead of her, skewered on her bowsprit, lay the New World.

CHAPTER 10

The *Santa Inez* drifted until the rising sun etched the contours of the land ahead against the skyline. De la Serena consulted the chart, which was amateurishly drawn, and labored to calculate their position. He sent two seamen forward with a depth line and orders to keep a sharp eye out for the mottled brown stain of approaching shoals.

"It is Hispaniola," de la Serena muttered repeatedly as he tried to match the island ahead with its crude image on the chart. While de la Serena pondered where they were, the *Santa Inez* jogged back and forth fretfully like a nervous bridegroom.

Eventually, de la Serena came to a decision and set a course that would take the ship toward the western tip of the land ahead and through the Windward Passage. On the charts the Windward Passage was marked as a zone of contrary winds, but he was hoping that the trades would continue to be favorable. His other choice was to go through the Mona Passage, which would take the *Santa Inez* on a longer, more roundabout way to Jamaica.

Among the sailors the sight of the landform looming ahead of the ship had sparked euphoria, and groups of them milled around the deck, chattering like children who had just suffered through the gloomy solemnities of High Mass on Easter Sunday. Everyone was suddenly in a good mood, and the surge of camaraderie led to some good-natured joshing and wrestling.

De la Serena called a public prayer, and the men quickly assembled in a somber line with their heads bowed, looking properly solemn as the ship owner gave voice to their thanks to God for allowing their ship to survive this long passage at sea.

Carlos bowed his head also, bitterly reflecting on this display of hypocrisy. He did not look at de la Serena during the recital of the prayer and wondered if anyone else on board knew the man's true feelings about religion.

After the prayer, the crew dispersed, some of the men continuing the lighthearted horseplay. Ahead of the surging ship the land swelled slowly in the morning sunlight, rising regally out of a bed of sparkling water, and the eye could make out a rangy green mountain towering above the seashore and wreathed at its foothills by a luxuriant forest. It was like watching a beautiful woman stepping slowly out of a bath and stretching herself, and the men alternated between babbling happily like children and simply staring at the lovely landform dripping with morning mist and sunrise dimness.

But the wind was contrary, and the *Santa Inez* was slowly forced to fall off until, in spite of her attempts to claw her way toward the Windward Passage, she nearly got caught in the irons, her sails flapping wildly, and had to reach parallel to the shore. With the land off her windward beam, the ship drove languidly through a calm sea crinkled with catpaws and the occasional groundswell where the ocean peeled off swollen mounds of water and sent them tumbling gently toward the shoreline like a caress. The wind held and before evening they could see the Mona Passage between Puerto Rico and Hispaniola exactly as it was marked on the crude map. But de la Serena did not want to attempt the passage with night falling, so he gave orders for the ship to heave to and wait out the darkness. Some of the men grumbled that they could have been ashore by now, but deep in their hearts, as much as they hungered to feel land under their feet, they knew that to lie offshore was prudent.

Night fell over the ship like a blanket suddenly dropping from the sky. One minute the earth was lit and the ocean and strange land off the beam of the ship bathed in the innocence of sunshine, and the next the whole world was blinded by a menacing darkness. The *Santa Inez* hove to, her sails flapping listlessly.

De la Serena doubled the watch, and dispatched two men with a depth line to sound out the bottom every hour on the hour.

Carlos came on watch at midnight. The land hulked in the darkness like a shipwreck, and in the distance the eye could make out none of its distinguishing features, seeing only a more solid lump of looming darkness.

"Do you know what that is, Carlos?" de la Serena asked in a conspiratorial whisper. "It is land unnamed. On the maps, its promontories and capes are blanks. Two hundred years from now, every piece of it, every mountain, every cove, will be named. Now it is terra incognito."

Carlos was unimpressed, and it showed in the piggish grunt that sprang from him in reply.

"Perhaps that should be Point de la Serena," the older man said. "Or why not Cape de la Serena? Or Mount de la Serena? Who would deny me Cove de la Serena?"

"Why not buy the whole Jamaica, then, señor, and give it your name?" Carlos muttered.

De la Serena did not hear the sarcasm in the seaman's tone. Perhaps it was the night or the long voyage that was coming to an end, but he eagerly seized on the suggestion and began to pace the poop deck in a spasm of excitement. "Who gave that island its name, anyway?" he asked speculatively, on his second turn around the deck. "I read that it was the Indians. What do they know? It is a word from their barbarous tongue. It is a word without meaning. Why shouldn't Jamaica be named *de la Serena*? There is no good reason! Can you think of one?"

"Other than local custom, no, señor," Carlos mumbled. He was not yet fully awake, being one of those people to whose senses sleep clings like a bedimming cobweb long after they've risen.

"It is a wonderful idea, Carlos," de la Serena breathed fervently, pausing in his agitated pacing. "I have read that unlike Hispaniola, Jamaica is doing poorly as a colony. I wonder who owns it."

Carlos grew sullen, regarding the whole conversation as a ridiculous daydream, so he said nothing lest he say the wrong thing. But the older man's eyes were burning at him in the flaring glow of the cresset as if expecting an answer.

"God?" he mumbled.

"There is no god, remember? It must be owned by the Columbus heirs and the Crown."

The vessel shuddered under them, and de la Serena looked quickly at Carlos.

"It is the wind that is shifting," Carlos said quickly. "Helmsman," he bawled down at the steering quarters, "hard astarboard!"

"Hard astarboard," the helmsman replied, his voice echoing from below deck.

The *Santa Inez* lumbered wheezily to the left, her sails spilling the wind and fluttering like beating wings.

In 1520, *hard astarboard* meant pushing the tiller to the right, which turned the ship to the left. This ridiculous misnomer continued until the ill-fated *Titanic* sank and the stupidity of ancient maritime terminology became public in the subsequent investigative hearings. But for now, to go to the left, the command was bellowed to the helmsman to push the tiller to the right.

In any event, once more the *Santa Inez* hove to—her head into the wind, her sails fluttering uselessly—and drifted listlessly under the night sky. Off her starboard beam, the unlit, hulking mass of Hispaniola loomed above the starlit sea, and in the distance they could hear the rattle of surf warning of an ironbound shoreline.

Daylight sprang on the ship like a hungry predator, and under the direction of de la Serena, she scooped up the wind in her trimmed sails and began jogging toward the Mona Passage. Off her port beam, the lumpy island of Puerto Rico crouched. Off her starboard, the whitened, stony claws of Hispaniola slid past. Ahead of the ship was Mona Island, impaled in the middle of the passage. The charts indicated an area of shoals radiating outward from the solitary island planted right in the center of the projected route of the ship. De la Serena set a course to keep the island on his starboard beam, and the *Santa Inez* driven by a favorable wind slipped through the passage. By nightfall, Mona Island was astern, and the *Santa Inez* had caught the local trades and was steering northeast for Jamaica.

Around the ship, instead of the barren emptiness of deep sea, the coastline of an edenic island—green and aromatic—opened like a wildflower. The breeze

smelled of land, and with every deep breath the crewmen filled their lungs with the fresh fragrance of creation. The waters under the ship teemed with life, and
so bountiful was the fishing that the cook respectfully
asked the men to land no more fish. Ahead of the ship,
Jamaica lay just below the horizon.

De la Serena kept a respectful distance between
his vessel and the coastline of Hispaniola. The charts
warned him of the approach of what would come to
be known as Cabo Beata and the Splinter of Beata—
a razor-sharp rock which thrusts a pointed lance offshore in a bed of shoals that threatens to rip open the
hull of any unwary ship.

The ship ghosted through the starry night to fresh
air as sharp and clear as mountain spring water, and
the intoxicating nearness of land so excited her crew
that many could not sleep and paced the deck restlessly, chattering eagerly like dickering moneylenders.

Soon the island stabbed the tusk of a green mountain out of the ocean, and the air was filled with the
fragrances of wildflowers and blossoming trees.

"It is Jamaica!" de la Serena announced joyfully to
all within earshot. Then he added wistfully to himself,
sotto voce, "One day may it be known as the Island of
de la Serena."

The *Santa Inez* did not know exactly where to go, and it
showed from her erratic movements that first morning
off the coastline of Jamaica. De la Serena had a vague

idea where the first settlement had been established. Somewhere on the north coast, near where his ship was at the moment, there was a settlement named Seville la Nueva—New Seville—but exactly where he did not know. He sent a man topside to the crow's nest to search for the settlement, promising a reward to the first sailor to spot it.

The ship behaved like a lost animal trying to find its burrow, nosing her way into coves, easing perilously close to the shoreline, and darting quickly out to sea again when the water became too shallow. She was zigzagging close to the shoreline like a fretful moth dancing around an open flame when the crow's nest lookout cried, "Señor! A boat!" and pointed to a canoe that had just cleared a cove and was heading out to sea.

There was a single person in the canoe, and he was propelling his craft with a piece of wood that he dipped into the water with a strange motion.

"Helmsman," de la Serena shouted, "helm hard aport!"

The *Santa Inez*, creaking and groaning with the sudden turn, came about sluggishly. The breeze was light and fitful, gusting from the land in teasing puffs, and if the person in the boat wanted to escape, all he had to do was turn around and head toward the shore, where the bigger vessel could not follow.

But he did not try to escape. He did just the opposite: he turned and headed directly toward the

Santa Inez, lifting up his hands and hoisting the steering wood overhead. Then he slid to his knees in the small boat and tried to bow low, nearly causing his craft to capsize. The men gathered at the railing of the ship and watched with amazement at the antics of the strange brown man headed for them in his odd-looking craft.

It was Orocobix. He was yelling in the Taíno language, "Gods from the sky, I believe! I believe!"

CHAPTER 11

Orocobix was fishing over a reef when he encountered the weary *Santa Inez*. He was fishing in the traditional Arawak way—with a remora he had captured months ago and kept alive in a bamboo pen in the shallows. The remora, transported aboard the canoe in a gourd of seawater, had been fed so little so that it was ravenously hungry and would fasten itself onto any passing prey. When Orocobix came to a place where there were fish, he would release the remora with a dyed cotton line tied to its tail. As soon as the remora had attached its suckers to a passing fish, he would pull them both into the boat. Then he would pry the remora off its prey by exposing it to the air where it could not breathe.

Since the death of Brayou, Orocobix had been living under a lingering sadness. Normally, he was lighthearted with all among whom he lived. Even the cacique, Datijao, found his good spirits infectious and often came to him seeking companionship when his own heart was heavy with his many responsibilities. Being the cacique, he had his own ceremonial *duho*—an elaborately carved stool that an attendant carried wherever the cacique went, so that he would always

have a seat befitting his dignity. This particular cacique did not like the responsibilities of his office, but
he had no choice, having inherited the throne from his
mother's line. He was no older than Orocobix, but in
these unusual times, his spirit always seemed weighted
down.

It was a time of change for his people, Datijao said,
and he admitted to Orocobix that he did not know
what to do. His was the only reign that had to face up
to cruel gods. What could anyone do if the gods were
evil?

The cacique asked Orocobix this question on the
night of the feast in remembrance of Brayou. He had
a puzzled look in his eyes, for he had been smoking
cohiba, and it had gone to his head. As usual he was
attended by four naked elders who dogged his every footstep, correcting him for any ceremonial flubs
and reminding their naked king constantly of the
high standard of behavior he was expected to follow.
That night, as the ceremonial feasting was coming to
an end, and during a moment when his advisers had
drifted off to celebrate with nearby friends, the cacique whispered to Orocobix, "I wish I could live like
you."

Orocobix did not understand why the cacique
would say something like that, but he thought perhaps he was under the influence of the cohiba. He had
no reply to such a comment, so he said nothing.

His eyes darting furtively at his clutch of advisers

who squatted nearby, the cacique sighed and mumbled, "What do you think about the gods from the sky
who walk among us, Orocobix?"

Orocobix was silent for a long moment, almost
to the point of rudeness, before he finally stirred and
said, "I believe that the gods are good and mean us no
harm."

"That is a good belief," the cacique whispered in
the voice of a fellow plotter. "Others say that they are
bad gods who must be resisted." He made a vague
motion with his head toward where his advisers sat in
a gossipy group, and Orocobix could almost hear the
voices of dissension shouting conflicting advice to the
young cacique.

"I will try to meet these gods myself and learn
about them," Orocobix quietly replied. "I will go fishing and perhaps meet one of the ships that fly and see
the gods face-to-face for myself."

"That is good," the cacique said, "because I have
seen them face-to-face and still do not understand
their nature."

A few remaining celebrants, sluggish from too
much food and revelry, were sprawled out drowsily
around the fire that licked at the darkness with a serpent's tongue. Here and there, in the roseate glow of
the flames, some couples lay entwined in their private
passions. Most people had drifted away to their *bohios*—
the round wooden houses built with poles driven in
the ground and lashed together with river withes and

vines and covered with a roof of palm fronds. Foraging among the drowsy celebrants sprawled on the ground were alcos—the small barkless dogs that squeaked like rats—hunting for scraps of discarded food. Occasionally, a drowsy reveler would slap irritably at one of the animals, sending it scurrying away squeaking.

Orocobix left the celebration and walked into a vast moonless night splattered with the pinpricks of numberless stars. The trail underfoot was dim but he had walked it so many times before that his feet saw what his eyes could not. All around him the lights of the *cocuyos*—small lightning bugs—flickered a blue glow in incomprehensible patterns.

The next morning he put out to sea in his small canoe.

De la Serena was like a child in his excitement and was openly brimming with delight as Orocobix paddled his canoe furiously toward the hove-to ship whose sails were flapping like the wings of an enormous sea bird. From every part of the ship, bored crew members streamed onto the deck of the *Santa Inez* to gaze with curiosity at the solitary figure who was paddling energetically toward them as though he feared they would flee.

"Gods from the sky," Orocobix occasionally cried over the effort of paddling the canoe, "wait for me!"

"Look at him," de la Serena chortled to no one in

particular, "he is a man of the New World. What is he saying, I wonder?"

The boatswain bellowed to the men gathered along the railing of the ship, "Anyone understand him?"

The string of seamen shook their heads.

Old Hernandez stepped forward. "George, the Englishman who is the cook's mate, has been to the New World and says he understands the Indians."

"George?" someone scoffed. "The one they call the magpie because of his constant chatter? If you listened to him, you'd believe he can talk even to birds!"

"Nevertheless," said old Hernandez, "this is his third trip to the Indies."

"Call him!" de la Serena said sharply.

The cry went up for the Englishman George, who emerged from the bowels of the ship, wiping his greasy hands on a soiled apron. He was a little man who stunk of the kitchen and yesterday's food, and his pale complexion was soft and puffy like that of a mushroom growing under a rotting log.

De la Serena looked him up and down. "You understand Indians?" he asked incredulously.

"Oh, yes, monsieur," George said with an ingratiating smile, inflating visibly with a show of self-importance before the watching crew. "This is my third trip to the Indies and I have learned their ways."

"Yes, yes," de la Serena said impatiently. "But can you understand their words?"

"Not every one of them, signor," George admitted,

adding quickly, "but enough of them to catch their meaning."

Orocobix, meanwhile, had clambered aboard the ship from his small canoe and was staring at the gods with open adoration. He threw himself facedown on the deck, prostrating himself just as Moses had done when he saw the burning bush.

"Gods from the sky, I know you are good. And I do believe," Orocobix said fervently. "I have come to serve you."

"What'd he say?" asked de la Serena.

"He said," George answered, "that he's most pleased to make your worship's acquaintance even though the weather has been foul lately."

De la Serena looked suspiciously at George. "Are you absolutely certain that's what he said?"

"No, not absolutely. But these people here are a funny lot. You have to learn to read between the lines, if you follow my meaning."

The seamen who gathered to gawk at Orocobix stirred restlessly. One of them touched him on the shoulder as if to verify that he was made, like them, of flesh. They saw standing naked before them a trim brown man in his early twenties, with dark glistening straight hair and a physique as well proportioned and sleek as that of a deep sea fish. His body was decorated all over with streaks of ocher, white, and red paint, his dark eyes burning with the glint of intelligence. Between his legs dangled his bare genitals under a ruff of wiry hair. The Spaniards around him, in contrast, looked gnomic, squat, and misshapen, like burrowing animals.

"He's as naked as when his mother bore him," murmured one seaman.

"Are the women also unclothed?" another asked hopefully.

Orocobix looked nervously from the face of one god to another and got to his feet slowly, his hands held palms-up in front of him to show that he had no weapon and had come in peace.

"Ask him if he knows where the settlement is," said de la Serena. "Sevilla la Nueva."

"Mmmm," George said, scratching a trail of soot across his grimy chin, "that's not easy."

He turned to Orocobix and practically shouted in his face, "Sevilla la Nueva. Where? Here? Or back there?"

Orocobix took a step backward and bowed from the waist. "You are the gods. Anything you want me to do, I will do."

George thought for a minute and then exclaimed, "Here, let's try this!"

He began an elaborate pointing all over the ship, meaning to indicate everyone aboard as well as the vessel itself, and then he pointed to the shoreline and gestured with his hands to show where they were headed. After some minutes of this pantomime, Orocobix gradually began to understand—the gods were looking for the dwellings of the other gods. He had never been there himself but he had rowed his canoe past it many times. His face lighting up with understanding, he pointed to the east where the land clubbed at the ocean with the blunt end of a distant promontory.

"He says it's over there," George announced, clapping Orocobix on the back.

With the canoe in tow, the *Santa Inez* caught a land breeze and ghosted up the coast. De la Serena took the breeze as a good sign, for it eased his fear of a deadly lee shore in strange waters. Nevertheless, he sent a grommet forward to keep a sharp lookout for shoals that splattered the clear water like the grimy handprints of children.

The *Santa Inez* rounded the promontory and sailed into a broad open bay in which several coastal vessels and one brigantine swung at anchor. Beyond the bay the land swept up a slope and furrowed into a dark green mountain. Scattered over the hillside were several small houses and buildings laid out in roughly a circular pattern. A tail of smoke curled into the air from one of the buildings, and one slope of the mountain range showed scribbles of a plow and other signs of cultivation.

It was impossible to say why, but from the point of view of the *Santa Inez*, the settlement was so crude and dilapidated that it seemed infected with the lassitude of malarial fever, and even so far out to sea, the men of the *Santa Inez* could feel the dispiritedness of the colony.

De la Serena, who had remained on the deck all day, said to George, "Ask the Indian the name of that settlement."

George pointed to the shoreline with its few buildings and a decrepit wharf, and raising his voice as if he was speaking to a deaf man, he bawled out, "What settlement name?"

Orocobix gestured to show humility and said in a prayerful voice, "I'm your servant. I will do anything you wish because I believe with all my heart that you are good, kind gods who will do me no wrong. Tell me what to do."

"Well?" snapped de la Serena.

"He says he's not sure, that the name keeps changing."

"I don't believe you understand a word of what he's saying," de la Serena said crossly. "Go back to your pots and pans."

"I do understand," yelped George, "although he's speaking with a funny accent. Nobody's perfect, you know."

"I said, get back to your station."

George retreated, grumbling that it was all unfair, and disappeared below deck. Orocobix glanced around him at the men, who were staring openly at him with intense curiosity.

Some of them were ogling his canoe, which was dug out from the trunk of a cotton tree and had no seams or joinery and no thwarts. A few of them were discussing his paddle, which they had never seen before although they were quite familiar with oars. Several of them seconded the opinion of Columbus that it resembled a baker's peel.

Orocobix, uncomfortable at being the center of attention, was nevertheless pleased. He was in the company of the gods, aboard their vessel that soared magically through the seas. They were good gods, just as he had thought. None of them had attempted to harm him. All of them were staring at him if they had never seen a man before.

"I wonder what he's thinking," de la Serena muttered to no one in particular.

"He thinks we're gods," Carlos said brashly.

"How can you tell?"

"Let me show you," Carlos replied in a strangely formal voice.

Stepping forward until he was face-to-face with Orocobix, Carlos pointed imperiously to the deck on which the two men stood. Orocobix stared at him fixedly before he understood.

He fell to his knees and prostrated himself before God Carlos. Orocobix did not know the tradition of kneeling and had no inkling of the various body positions used by European Christians to signal self-abasement. But the posture he struck was a universal one that required no interpretation—one human being groveling abjectly at the feet of another. Some of the seamen took a step forward as if to help Orocobix stand, but the eyes of Carlos the murderer flashed a warning.

With a ceremonial flourish, the Spaniard extended an arm out to Orocobix like a king bidding a servile subject to rise. As the men gaped in disbelief, the Indian came slowly to his feet, his eyes burning with a worshipful adoration which, if the scene had been portrayed in the overwrought religious art of the sixteenth century, would have earned Orocobix the painted gold halo of an angel or saint.

"Am I not his god?" Carlos chortled with triumph.

"This is blasphemous," old Hernandez grumbled.

"Prepare to drop anchor," de la Serena ordered.

The crew scrambled to their various posts, some manning the tangled ropes that controlled the sails, others readying the anchor rode.

Scruffy and weather-beaten, the *Santa Inez* limped gingerly into Santa Gloria Bay on the north coast of Jamaica.

CHAPTER 12

On the vastness of the ocean, an island often seems like a blur in a daydream. But this island looming over the *Santa Inez* was crowned with burly mountains full of the solid substance and vivid color found only in wakefulness. It was so lush and green that the eyes of the crew—used to the monotonous blue of the deep—lingered lovingly over its folds and pleats as though finding newly discovered treasures. Near the shore a poinciana tree in full bloom was afire with gaudy red blossoms.

Her crew chattered excitedly like a flock of roosting parrots as the *Santa Inez* anchored in the middle of the bay near the brigantine. De la Serena changed into his shore clothes and began pacing the deck irritably.

"How do they know that we're not pirates?" he fumed. "We could be an enemy ship! No challenge! No warning shot. No official on hand to examine our papers. What kind of colony is this?"

"We flew a friendly flag when we sailed in," old Hernandez said mildly. "They know we are not the enemy."

"Anyone could capture such an island!" de la Serena raved.

His words would prove prophetic. In 1655 an English expedition, after failing to take Cuba on the orders of Oliver Cromwell, would fall on defenseless Jamaica like a lion on a foundling. In a matter of only months the Spanish would be driven from the land, leaving behind them, after an occupation of over 150 years, a handful of names that still cling like burrs to some few rivers and towns: Ocho Rios, Rio Bueno, Savanna la Mar, Mount Diablo, Rio Cobre, and in a supreme irony, the Anglicized name of what used to be the island's capital under the Spaniards—Spanish Town.

But this would not happen for 135 years and by then all souls, the fretful and the uncaring, alive in 1520 would be wiped off the face of the earth.

"A boat approaches," a seaman called out.

De la Serena rushed to the side of the ship and saw two men in a battered rowboat pulling up alongside the *Santa Inez*. A resplendent young man climbed aboard with some effort and looked around at the gawking crew. He wore a uniform decorated with ribbons and rosettes and a cockaded hat that might have been the crest on the head of an extinct prehistoric bird.

"My name is Juan Mazuelo," he announced officiously, snapping the heels of his boots together and touching the brim of his ridiculously ornate hat. "I am the personal secretary of the alcade of Jamaica. What ship is this and what is your business?"

"I am Alonso de la Serena, and this is the *Santa Inez*,

my ship," came the sharp reply followed by the sound of knuckles banging with the authority of ownership against the cabin.

"Are you under a commission?"

"This is a privately owned vessel on a voyage of exploration," de la Serena said stiffly. "I request permission to land and to have an audience with the alcade."

"We were hoping you were a supply ship. We are sorely in need of supplies," said the secretary.

De la Serena took the man aside and invited him down to his private quarters. An hour later, the two men emerged from the cabin, guffawing and looking a little wobbly.

Bidding de la Serena goodbye as though he were parting from an old friend, the official climbed over the side, got into the rowboat, and set out for the shore.

"How did he do that?" the boy Pedro whispered.

"He got him drunk and bribed him," old Hernandez grunted cynically.

"Prepare to tow the ship to the pier," de la Serena ordered.

The men ran out the long boat, which the *Santa Inez* carried upside down on her forward deck. A line was attached to the ship's anchor bitt and she was towed slowly to shore and tied up at the end of the pier.

Ahead of her, nestled on a gently sloping stretch of land, was Sevilla la Nueva, New Seville, Spain's frail toehold in Jamaica.

* * *

In 1520 New Seville existed mainly as a drawing, where it was laid out according to the royal grid plan first used in the construction of Santa Fe, Spain, and later in building the towns of Santa Domingo in Hispaniola and Caparra in Puerto Rico.

Overlooking the bay, the town was discreetly set back in the foothills so that pirates and other marauders would have difficulty bombarding its buildings from the sea. The settlement, in spite of its ambitious name, consisted of only an incomplete government building, a masonry church, a clutch of small houses and commercial buildings, a few storage sheds, and a crude wooden barracks for a garrison of soldiers.

However splendid it looked on paper, the real New Seville was a settlement of dour poverty and wretchedness. Its streets were little more than mud-lined trails tamped down and made smooth by the hooves of animals and the feet of men. Clinging to the sloping land was a sparse collection of buildings constructed of masonry and wood.

There was no parade of horse-drawn carriages, no promenading of the gentry showing off their elegant silks and satins like preening peacocks; no elaborate town square with statues of dead European butchers; no memorials to victories and slaughter; no hint that here was an outpost of a mighty empire with a heritage of discovery and conquest. There was only a grubby starkness befitting the breeding ground of a colony of migrating locusts.

The signs of hardship, boredom, and want were everywhere—in the dinginess of the houses, the griminess of the land, the stultified expressions on the faces of uncurious passersby and indifferent loiterers. Everyone and everything seemed to sag and droop with a noticeable weariness.

The crew of the *Santa Inez* found a shack that served as a makeshift cantina and settled in to get drunk. A few Spaniards were strewn throughout the room, which was streaked with bad light and reeked of the laborers' stench. The bar owner's wife, fat and slovenly and desperately in need of a bath, was the only female in sight.

"Where are all the women?" asked a seaman.

"There are plenty of Indian women to be had," the bartender said with an ugly leer. "Just grab one and take her in the bush."

"This is what I came over three thousand miles to see?" growled the boatswain.

No one answered him.

Carlos was not particularly eager to go ashore. Some seamen need transition time to get accustomed once more to land, and he was one of them. He preferred to slowly ease into land like a swimmer who enters a body of cold water toe first. So, before lots could be drawn to see who would stay on the ship and who would go ashore, Carlos volunteered to stay aboard. The boy Pedro said he would also stay.

One of the reasons Carlos remained behind was to play with Orocobix, who kept pointing to the sky in their discussions, convinced that the myth of the sky gods had come true with the arrival of these strangers. So he followed Carlos everywhere, watching the god closely to understand how gods think and what they want.

He was amazed to find that the gods and the Arawaks more or less did the same things throughout the day, such as eating, sleeping, and relieving themselves. He followed every move Carlos made and studied what he did and why. Occasionally, he would ask a question, but the god would not understand him and he would get no sensible reply.

Carlos offered the Indian something to eat, but Orocobix declined. Later, assuming the air of a proud proprietor, Carlos led the Indian on a tour of the ship, showing off its mysteries. He showed Orocobix one of the four Lombard cannons the *Santa Inez* carried for defense, making it clear through gestures and pantomiming that this was an implement of death and destruction. He demonstrated this power by making a booming noise, slapping the muzzle of the weapon, and then pretending to fall before its onslaught of deadly shot.

Orocobix did not understand at first, but he soon grasped the significance of this particularly ugly piece of metal. Using gestures, Carlos told the Indian to try and lift the cannon. Orocobix did and found that he

could not move it even an inch, it was so heavy. He
had never seen metal before, and he rubbed the thick
muzzle of the cannon slowly as if he were caressing it.

"Thunder stick," he said in Taíno, looking impressed.

"Sí! Sí!" Carlos agreed affably.

Savoring the awed expression on the Indian's face,
Carlos showed him a crossbow, and when Orocobix
did not understand its use, Carlos fired a bolt that
flew over the deck and sank deep into a piling with
a loud thwack. For the next twenty minutes Carlos
struggled to retrieve it. He ended up digging out the
metal bolt with his knife.

Carlos then showed Orocobix a harquebus, which
belonged to the *Santa Inez*. One of the first handguns
ever invented, the harquebus was like a miniature cannon, it was so heavy, and its firing gave off a deafening
sound and required the help of several men. Orocobix dimly understood that this was another thunder
stick, and as he and Carlos gabbled in languages that
the other did not understand, the Arawak shuffled
throughout the ship looking cowed by the power and
might of the gods' possessions.

It was a hot day, and growing bored, Carlos decided for fun to teach the Indian a trick. The two men
communicated with crude gestures and miming, and
at first it was difficult for Orocobix to understand
what the god wanted him to do. Finally, the god made
it plain that what he wanted was for Orocobix to fall
on his knees and bow down low before him at the

snap of his fingers. To the Indian, it was a strange game for a god to enjoy but one he was quite willing to play for the god's pleasure.

The boy Pedro did not like this game because he thought it blasphemous, but he held his tongue for fear of angering Carlos. So for the rest of the first day, he watched quietly as Carlos strutted up and down the deck snapping his fingers as a signal for the Indian to bow down low before him like a Muslim at prayer and to rise again at a gesture of his hand.

From a distance, the Arawak and the Spaniard might have seemed as if they were performing a complex mating dance, complete with curtsying and bowing, on the deck of the battered, tied-up ship. Carlos would swagger past the Indian, turn, and snap his fingers. Orocobix would immediately fall on the deck in the prostrated stance of a groveller. The Spaniard would use his hands to indicate that the Indian could now rise, which he would, looking hard at Carlos for another cue. All this was possible because the Arawaks were a bright people with a natural gift of mimicry. As Columbus cold-bloodedly wrote about the Arawaks in his journal, *"They ought to make good and skilled servants, for they repeat very quickly whatever we say to them."*

It was an endless, pointless, stupid game—or so it seemed to the boy Pedro, who finally blurted out in a moment of brashness, "Carlos, why do you do this thing?"

"Why not?" Carlos mumbled. "There is no harm in it."

Orocobix strained to understand what the two gods were saying, but he couldn't quite grasp their meaning.

Next, the Spaniard taught the Indian to say "God Carlos," until he was able to say the words so that anyone would understand them. To test this, Carlos called out to the boy Pedro, who was now walking on the beach, and when the boy came running, Orocobix solemnly faced him and said, "God Carlos, God Carlos, God Carlos," until the god ordered him to stop with a gesture.

"Did you understand that?" Carlos asked excitedly.

"Yes," the boy Pedro whispered, "but you're not God. You've taught him a lie."

"To him I am God," Carlos boasted. Then he snapped his fingers and Orocobix fell on his knees and prostrated himself on the deck. "See!"

"I do not think this is right, Carlos," Pedro whispered, hanging his head as if he'd just witnessed something shameful.

Carlos chuckled. He thought it was very funny. Orocobix remained prone on the deck, awaiting the hand signal from God Carlos to rise.

During the night only a few men returned to the ship, most preferring instead to sleep on solid ground. Many by then were drunk and found a tree to curl up under; others rented a sleeping pallet in a dirty, makeshift inn run by a Portuguese settler. Sometime around midnight, de la Serena returned to the ship and went down the companionway to his bed—the only one on the *Santa Inez*.

At daybreak Carlos awoke to find his worshipper curled up two feet away, staring at him intently. Yawning and stretching, the two men peered at the sunrise as if they were mystified to find themselves still on the earth. The boy Pedro lay nearby, asleep.

Carlos was becoming annoyed at the constant attentiveness of his worshipper. Yesterday it was flattering, but now as he woke up he was beginning to find the Indian irksome. He couldn't ask the naked creature about anything that required more than pointing and miming. And when he did frame a question with elaborate gestures, the sign-answers he got in reply were barely comprehensible.

As the dawn light spread across the sky, Carlos stood up on the foredeck and looked around him. It was a windless morning, and although the sun had not yet cleared the horizon, the clamminess of a whore's loveless wet kiss hung over the bay. In the distance, an Arawak fishing canoe was passing. Orocobix was staring at the god keenly, expectantly, like a puppy who wanted to continue yesterday's play.

Carlos abruptly pointed to the sea and indicated to Orocobix that he should get in his canoe and go. The Arawak did not understand at first that the god was sending him away.

"Oh, God," he said to God Carlos in a supplicating voice, "I long to understand your words and will obey them all if only you would teach me their meaning."

"I said, get off!" Carlos roared, gesticulating to show what he wanted the Arawak to do.

Orocobix, although he now understood, did not move. Carlos grabbed him by the hair and shoved him brutally off the *Santa Inez* and onto the pier.

"Now you stay there!" God Carlos commanded.

Orocobix clambered to his feet and tried to step back aboard the ship.

"Stay there!" Carlos screamed, pushing the Indian back onto the pier. Orocobix fell to his knees in the prostrated position and seemed to be begging for mercy.

The shouting woke up a few of the hungover men who were strewn asleep all over the deck in curled-up lumps of flesh and clothing. Groggy and drowsy, a few of them propped their heads up on their hands to watch. A couple of them grumbled about the noise but no one made a move to intervene.

Orocobix did not understand. "Why does the god treat me so harshly?" he asked pitifully from the pier, holding out his arms as if he would embrace his god.

"I do not think, Carlos," the boy Pedro muttered, "that you should do these things to one who worships you."

"I'm tired of playing with him," Carlos snarled.

"I'll go for now, but I will return," said Orocobix sadly after he had been roughly thrown off the ship for the fourth time. Then he shuffled off to his tied-up

canoe, looking forlorn and rejected and pausing frequently to turn and see whether Carlos had changed
his mind. The god had not; so the Indian rowed away
and headed out to open sea.

Orocobix was paddling away when de la Serena
appeared on deck, looking around as if he'd lost something.

"Who was shouting?" he asked a drowsy seaman
sprawled out on the poop deck.

"It was God Carlos sending the Indian away," he
responded sleepily. But he did not say it too loudly for
fear Carlos would hear. And before he settled down
again to catch another snatch of sleep, the seaman
glanced around to be sure that Carlos was not nearby.

"What a dismal place this colony is," de la Serena
moaned.

CHAPTER 13

Shortly after the *Santa Inez* made her landfall, de la Serena fell mysteriously sick, leaving the crew fretting that their captain would die and they would be abandoned in the New World. Feverish, he lay abed in a grubby little room in the makeshift inn whose walls were stained with sooty candle smudges and whose single window was smothered under a soiled bedsheet that served as a crude curtain. Here, at the ends of the earth, he lay sprawled out on a narrow homemade bed under a frayed dirty blanket, haunted by his wife's prophecy on the pier that he would die and be buried unmourned among strangers in the New World. That she might be proven right galled him more than the prospect of dying itself.

A physician, who was also the settlement's barber, was summoned to his sickbed where, after prodding and poking him with thick, greasy fingers, he announced gravely that de la Serena had to undergo bleeding or he would die.

Bleeding—opening a vein in the patient's arm and drawing off a quantity of blood to reduce the imbalance of so-called humors—was a standard sixteenth-century medical treatment for virtually every disease.

And although de la Serena had no reason to think the practice the quackery that it was, he had bad memories of previous bleedings that had left him breathless and weak.

He refused the treatment, dismissed the physician, and sweated out the fever, which came and went capriciously, gradually abated, and eventually disappeared. One morning he woke up weak but free of fever and was able to eat for the first time in days.

Without knowing it, de la Serena had weathered *the seasoning*—as the initial perilous days of acclimatizing to Jamaica later came to be called. For the first three centuries of the island's occupation, the mortality rate of new arrivals to Jamaica was so ghastly that one writer characterized the island as "a vast graveyard." A classic example was the arrival in December 1656 of 1,600 colonists who settled near Morant Bay. By March of 1657, a scant three months later, 1,200 were dead, including the leader and his wife. Responsible for this indiscriminate slaughter was yellow fever spread by the mosquito. Later, medical science would find that while whites had no immunity to this disease, blacks often had a natural resistance that enabled them to better adapt to life in the West Indies.

De la Serena thought often during those days of the fever that he, too, would die. But death held no terror for him, for he believed that it would return him to the unknowing void which had spawned him. And, being a logical man, since he believed that after

death he would have no more memory of having existed than an adobe brick, he did not find such an end
fearful.

But once the fever broke and he was out of bed, de
la Serena became nearly overwhelmed by a feeling of
absurdity about what he was doing in such a remote
and desolate part of the world. He wondered what
could have possessed him to make such a long, pointless voyage, and for a day or two he moped like one
who had lost his life's purpose. But as he grew stron-
ger, his spirits rebounded and once again he became
determined to imprint his name on this new land.

How were geographical features of a newly discovered land named? On the daily walks he took
to regain his strength, de la Serena pondered this
question as if it were a holy mystery. Obviously
there was some protocol at work that he did not
know. What he knew was common knowledge: all
explorers, including Columbus, felt free to name
lands that they encountered. But many explorers
named only the most conspicuous features of their
discoveries, leaving other geographical scraps unnamed. It did not occur to de la Serena that a land
already occupied by an indigenous people was not
unknown and therefore could not be discovered—
that claim of its discovery was based on an underly-
ing presumption that nothing existed unless known
to Europeans.

With his strength flooding back, de la Serena plotted

his next move. He made an appointment to see the alcade of Sevilla la Nueva.

The alcade, an official roughly equivalent to a governor, was responsible for the maintenance and upkeep of a new colony as well as for ensuring that the Crown received its share of any discovered wealth.

At the time of the arrival of the *Santa Inez* in 1520, the appointed alcade of Sevilla la Nueva was one Juan Caro, a brownnoser from Castile who had lobbied hard for an administrative position in a colony of the New World. He had done so in the mistaken belief that to be an alcade in the Indies would shower him with glory and renown. Wild rumors about the vast wealth of the Indies were then in circulation throughout Spain, and every young man with an adventurous heart hungered for a colonial posting.

A lanky man with a potbelly incongruous for one of his build, Juan Caro had gotten his position in a way commonplace for the times—through his connections to the court of Charles I, grandson of Ferdinand of Aragon and Isabella of Castile, the original sponsors of Columbus's explorations.

Juan Caro had said a word about his ambition to an important uncle who was owed a large sum of money by a spendthrift grandee highly placed among the brilliant courtiers who kept the twenty-year-old Charles I amused. The uncle murmured to the indebted courtier, who whispered to his mistress, who breathed the name of Juan Caro to the wife of the official on the board in charge of employing the alcades, and through this capillary seepage of influence, the appointment was secured.

It was an act that Caro bitterly regretted. He had been at the post now for eighteen months and had never detested a country or people more passionately. He was not enchanted by the lush green fields or the rolling hills or the loveliness of the clear blue ocean. The gentleness of the Indians he regarded as laziness and weakness. Nothing about his position interested him, and he had already begun the reverse process of having himself recalled through the same uncle's influence.

De la Serena found the alcade squatting morosely behind a desk made of rough-hewn lumber, his office little more than a dark burrow in a building that seemed to slump against the hillside. Caro knew the name and reputation of de la Serena, for like every brownnoser then or now, he had a keen nose for the smell of money and could tell that the elderly man sitting before him was rich. Trying his best to disguise his hatred of his present life, the alcade struggled to be cordial.

"You mean to tell me, señor, that you sailed all the way from Spain to this godforsaken island for no other reason but sightseeing?" Caro exclaimed with astonishment after listening to de la Serena's jumbled tale about having the desire to see the New World before he died.

De la Serena glanced around the empty room as if he suspected that eavesdroppers lurked nearby.

"No, señor," he whispered as though he told a shameful secret, "I do have another reason. I am seeking a legacy. I would like some part of this new land to be named after me."

A foxy gleam shining in his eyes, the alcade stared at the old man. "I do not understand what you mean, señor."

"You go into the interior and find a river you've never seen before. What name do you give it?"

The alcade thought about the question. "Of course," he said blandly, "everything in this island already has an Indian name. But we pay no attention to it. They call it one thing, and we call it another."

"And whose name prevails?"

"The one who has writing, iron, and gunpowder."

The two Spaniards chuckled.

"I should also warn you to hide your dead from the Indians, señor," the alcade said softly. "They think we are gods and cannot die. It is to our advantage to encourage them in this belief."

"Dead? We have no dead."

"You will. This is a place of death."

De la Serena lapsed into a pensive silence. Finally, he stirred as if awakening from a sleep. "Then, have all the mountains been named?"

"Señor, all the mountains have not even been explored. This is a big island and it is filled with mountains. We do not even know what kind of animals live on it. We do not know if there are venomous snakes or poisonous insects. We only know what the Indians have told us and what we have learned for ourselves."

"So there are many physical features still to be named," sighed de la Serena happily.

"There are countless unnamed promontories, districts, mountains, rivers, and for all we know, there may be nameless inland lakes or volcanoes."

De la Serena rubbed his hands together with the eager anticipation of a banker about to fondle a stack of newly minted money. "And who gives a new mountain its name?"

Caro thought for a moment. "I suppose the one who first finds it. But," he added hastily, "that name would have to be approved by the official in charge."

"Which is you."

A smile creased the alcade's face. He leaned forward expectantly. "A cartographer in our company is to begin a survey of the island soon and will draw a new map. I will speak to him about your wishes."

The two men stared at each other with a deep understanding.

"I would be grateful for that favor. And I'm a man who knows how to express gratitude."

"That is obvious, señor," Caro the brownnoser said smoothly, a greedy smile oozing over his face.

That very afternoon de la Serena was introduced to

the cartographer. He was a gloomy Frenchman of a nervous disposition who was always twitching. Everyone called him *Monsieur*, which was the only name by which he was known. He took his responsibilities very seriously and seemed to be overawed by the task of mapping Jamaica.

On the first meeting, Monsieur took de la Serena on a walk up a hill that offered a wide and expansive view of the bay above which the settlement was being built. It was a hard climb for an old man who had just recovered from being so ill, and it took longer to reach the summit than the Frenchman was used to, which made him irritated.

"Can't you go any faster?" he asked de la Serena peevishly when the older man kept falling behind.

"I've just recovered from the fever," de la Serena panted, leaning against a tree. "Go ahead of me. I will catch up."

"If you cannot keep up with me, how can you expect to catch up with me?"

De la Serena stared sternly at the man. "Is this the kind of respect you show your alcade's guests?" he asked sharply.

Realizing that he'd gone too far, Monsieur suddenly changed his attitude. He sat down heavily beside de la Serena.

"I'm sorry, señor," he muttered, wiping his sweaty face. He looked around the thick woodland that surrounded them. "It is this bestial country. It makes a

man forget civility. One cannot live among savages
without becoming one himself."

A raucous mob of screeching parrots suddenly
swooped into the surrounding trees, rippling the foliage with quivering spasms of iridescence like the
ocean crinkling in a breeze.

"Get along with you, you nasty creatures!" shouted
Monsieur, shaking his fist at the trees.

With a loud cackling, the flock fluttered off into
the woods. Monsieur watched them go.

"I hate birds," he said bitterly. "They have the perspective that I, a mapmaker, need but can never have.
It is up there that your eye clearly sees the topography
of the land. What can it be but a flaw in creation to
give such a perspective to a useless bird?"

"It is one of the many accidents of life," de la Serena murmured.

"It is the fault of God," grumbled the Frenchman.

The two men struggled up the slope until they
came to a scenic overlook. Below them spread the vista
of inlets and coves as the shoreline furled against the
ocean in irregular twists and furrows like a crumpled
edge of a hastily shed garment. Where the land met
the sea, the coastline was unevenly pleated. Stretched
immediately below them was Santa Gloria Bay, above
which Sevilla la Nueva rose in a sprinkle of buildings.

Sitting in the shade of a tree, they discussed the
difficulties of mapping a new land. The main problem,
said Monsieur, was that a cartographer saw the world

like a rabbit—from ground level. He had to translate
this horizontal view of the shoreline into its flat aerial
equivalent on paper, as if he shared the overhead perspective of the cursed bird. Drawing such a map accurately was a heavy burden.

"There is not even an available ship to take me
around the island. Yet I'm supposed to map it within
six months," whined the Frenchman.

"I have a ship," announced de la Serena. "She
needs to be careened. But when she is ready, I myself
would like to see the island."

"For what? To have a mountain named after you?
What is the reason for such a senseless ambition?"

"So I'm remembered after I'm dead," de la Serena
said softly.

"There is a better way," crowed the Frenchman.
"Don't die."

"What're you saying, Monsieur?" de la Serena
asked, looking perplexed.

"I have noticed that people who die are those who
agree to die. I do not agree to die. So I will not die."

"Señor, you're mistaken," de la Serena said firmly.
"You will die whether or not you agree to it. Nothing
can prevent eventual death."

"Prove that."

"It is common knowledge, señor."

"No, señor. It is a common superstition that
passes for knowledge. I oppose dying. And I will not
do it."

"You will die when your time comes," said de la Serena with quiet conviction.

"No, señor. I'm against this waste of human life. Death cannot happen without one's consent. And I will never consent."

De la Serena stared hard at the Frenchman, trying to decide whether he was joking. The Frenchman met his gaze without flinching.

"That is a mad opinion, señor."

The Frenchman shrugged like one who had heard this so many times before that it had become wearying. "So have a mountain named after you and then die. As for me, I prefer to remain alive."

"I regret to say that we're both destined to become dust."

"You may become dust, if you like. I choose to remain flesh." With that, Monsieur abruptly stood up, rubbed his belly languidly, and indicated that he was ready to return to the settlement. De la Serena trailed after him, half sliding and half walking down the steep, twisting footpath.

At the bottom of the hill de la Serena said, "When my ship is ready, she is still yours for circumnavigating the island, señor."

"You do not mind sailing with a cartographer who holds mad opinions?"

"Not if he will name a mountain after me."

The two men dusted themselves off and trudged toward the settlement. "What a pity you must die, señor," Monsieur chuckled sympathetically, "when death can be so simply avoided."

"I'm a hopeless traditionalist," de la Serena moaned sarcastically.

"A pity," murmured the Frenchman. "Such a pity."

CHAPTER 14

The gods were inconstant and changeable as the land breeze, and because no one could understand their words, speaking with them was a troublesome task.

In the flicker of the open fire, the old, creased faces aglow with the reddish tint of freshly boiled lobster remained impassive. One or two of the elders looked sympathetic and stirred as if moved to offer consolation to the speaker.

It was the first time Orocobix had been invited to address the elders at their council. Word about his visit to the craft belonging to the gods of the sky had spread throughout the village and reached the elders, who had summoned him to come and tell them what he had learned. And they were listening to him respectfully, for he was known to them since infancy as one whose heart was truthful.

Orocobix told the hushed elders about God Carlos, the one god he had come to know, of the god's strange hunger for signs of worship and respect, of his changeable nature and how the god had abruptly exiled him for no offense.

Calliou, one of the youngest and most hot-blooded

of the elders said, "This is not like a god, but a man. He is no god."

"He is a god," Orocobix nodded confidently.

"Show us this sign of respect that the god taught you," prompted another elder whose nickname was "Peacemaker" because he was always trying to soothe any hard feelings that arose among disputing tribe members. "Perhaps it is not what you think."

Orocobix demonstrated. First, he snapped his fingers like God Carlos did; then he fell on his knees and prostrated himself facedown on the floor. Next he showed the contemptuous hand gesture with which the god bid him to rise.

When he was finished, the elders sat quietly thinking, and there was no sound but the occasional bubbling of a full belly and the fire gnawing on the wood pile like a noisy rodent.

"Only vain men require such signs of humility from other men," said Calliou.

"No," Orocobix said sharply. "They are gods. They are not like you and me. They have strange implements and powers. They eat bitter food. Their vessel flies on the wind."

He described the thunder stick and the crossbow and other wonders whose rightful names he did not know but whose magic he himself had witnessed. He spoke of the immensity of their vessel and the intricate tangle of its rigging. He described the iron of the cannon, which was unlike any wood known to his father's father, harder even than stone.

One doubtful elder protested that nothing was harder than stone, that Orocobix exaggerated. Orocobix replied that he could only describe what his eyes had seen and that anyone who did not believe could visit the gods for himself and find out what magical powers they truly possessed.

The ring of elders fell silent and there was no movement except flickering shadows that writhed and danced to the flames of the crackling wood.

"It does not matter whether they are powerful men or gods," said another elder quietly. "Everyone knows what they do to our women. Evil is evil, whether done by gods or by men."

"We can kill men," observed Calliou sensibly, "but we cannot kill gods."

"We have tried to kill them before," said Peacemaker. "It is not easy to do."

Another elder repeated the story that had come down to the tribe. One day a long time ago—no one could say when—the gods from the sky suddenly appeared off the coast of Xamaca in their strange vessels. (It was 1494, the second voyage of Columbus.) Thinking them a new enemy, warriors poured down to the landing beach and attacked the invaders. But the gods rained down thunder and lightning on the Arawaks, slaying several warriors on the beach. Then the gods unleashed a pack of enormous, ferocious dogs no Arawak had ever seen before that savagely mauled the warriors, who fled in a crazed panic.

"I was there that day," said one elder faintly. "I have bitter memories of it."

Like all the others at the council, this elder—sitting with his legs crossed—was naked. Now he stood up unsteadily, for he was a very old man, and he opened his legs to reveal the teeth marks the dogs had tattooed that day on the soft flesh of his thighs near his stringy, wrinkled genitals.

The elders gaped at the wound, many shuddering as they imagined their own flesh being pierced by dog teeth in such a tender place.

Another long silence ensued.

"They are gods," Orocobix muttered. "And I do not believe they are wicked."

A mood of uncertainty fluttered over the council, and someone sighed as if longing for a time before these days of complexity and trouble—a sound so heartfelt and mournful that it might have come from any one of these sad fretful old Arawak elders struggling to understand their people's latest calamities.

Aside from being a settlement of want, boredom, and poverty, New Seville was also a cauldron of merciless heat. Every day was as blistering as the one before. The town itself was tucked in a stitch of coastline that turned and twisted like the scribble of a child. Farther up the coast, breezes blew daily, cooling the land with the clean smell of the ocean. But because of the chis-

eled cut of the landform and the hulking presence of
the mountains, no breezes blew over Santa Gloria Bay,
and man, beast, and land were steeped in the relentless stillness of an airless tomb.

Every afternoon the heat became so terrible that
the heavens exploded in bone-jarring peals of thunder as a blackness more menacing than the darkest
night curdled against the mountains and torrential
rain exploded across the bay. It was a tepid rain that
did not relieve or freshen but merely coated man and
beast with the sticky wetness of warm mouthwater.
Then the detonation of thunder would lessen and the
sun would come out and begin licking the bay with
a dog's warm tongue, spreading a sticky sweet mist
over the land.

"If I were a god," Carlos muttered to the boy Pedro
as they huddled under a tree for protection from one
of these thunderstorms, "I would not make it so hot."

"But you are not a god, señor," the boy replied
boldly.

Carlos cuffed him sharply on the side of the head.

The boy flinched and mumbled, "That still does
not make you a god, señor."

For several days, even as de la Serena lay recovering
on his sickbed, the *Santa Inez* was careened on a nearby
beach.

To careen a wooden ship meant hauling her up on
the land and using ropes to pull her over on her side,

exposing her wooden bottom to the sky for the crew to scrub and scrape off barnacles and algae. Then the seams between her planks, opened up by shipworms, teredos, and the constant pounding of the waves, would be recaulked and sealed. Careening had to be performed regularly to keep a wooden vessel afloat. Otherwise, she would take on water and sink.

Lying on her side, the *Santa Inez* looked like a beached sea monster, her masts and rigging sticking across the beach like lifeless tentacles while the crew swarmed over her and cleaned and scraped her rounded bottom. In the relentless heat, all the crew, even the cook, took part. The work was dirty, hard, and hot, and many of the men suffered cuts and splinters on their fingers and dripped bloody spots over the gristly underbelly of the beached ship.

Then the ship's carpenter, aided by the boy Pedro and another grommet, Alonzo, went to work on making the seams watertight. Using a caulking iron and mallet, the carpenter pounded strips of oakum into the openings between the planks and sealed the newly stuffed slits with a coat of hot pitch. Within minutes of clambering atop the exposed bottom of the ship, the caulking crew was drenched in sweat and speckled with splotches of tar and shreds of oakum.

One afternoon as the men huddled for shelter from a thunderstorm cannonading the bay with deafening salvos, they glimpsed an Indian woman crouching behind a leafy tree. At the sight of the gods from the sky, the woman froze like a stalked fawn, but when she realized that they had seen her, she leaped to her feet and hurried through the thicket, casting looks of terror over her shoulder. The men caught her, threw her to the ground, pried open her legs, and took turns on top of her while all around them the thunderstorm rumbled like an avalanche of boulders.

Her screams, shrill and discordant, pierced the woodland over the sounds of the storm like the cries of a crazed bird. When he realized what was happening, Carlos left the boy Pedro and old Hernandez under a tree and hurried to take his turn atop the woman.

"What are they doing to her?" the boy Pedro asked in a frightened voice.

"What men do to women," old Hernandez said gruffly.

"What is that? And why do you not do it also, señor?"

"Because I'm too old for such things."

"Will I do it also when I become a man?"

"Not if you grow into a good man."

They fell silent and listened grimly to the sobs and wails of the woman mixed incongruously with the sound of rain that seemed to come from a million unseen mouths howling in chorus.

Then, abruptly, the screaming stopped and only the rain and the fretful drumming of thunder against the mountains could be heard. Carlos, looking muddy and soiled like a hog after wallowing, returned to sit beside old Hernandez and the boy Pedro. Both shied away from him, for to the old man, Carlos stank of barnyard rutting, and to the boy Pedro, of a strange, raw musk.

Old Hernandez remained in a crouch and said nothing. The boy Pedro, who looked as if a question would explode out of him, squirmed and also made no remark.

Soon the rain was over and the men trooped out of the woodland and across the beach and swarmed once more over the dark bottom of the ship.

Later that day, as the twilight thickened around them, the men slogged wearily for the settlement where most of them would sleep outdoors.

One of them who had participated in the rape suddenly said, "What will we do if she makes a complaint against us?"

"We should have finished her off," muttered a second. "Now the authorities may send soldiers to find us."

"It's her fault for going around naked as a baby," a third complained. "What else can they expect? We are men."

"She was going around that way long before you left Cádiz," said old Hernandez.

"Shut up, old man," the complainer snapped.

"Do not tell me to shut up, señor," warned old Hernandez. "I will speak as freely as I please."

"Then," replied the man, "perhaps I will have to shut you up."

"You are welcome to try, señor," said old Hernandez, coming to a stop and turning to face the seaman.

For a brief moment, the two men faced each other threateningly. But the younger man saw something deadly in the eyes of old Hernandez that made him pause. He suddenly broke off and walked away, saving face by saying, "I do not fight with men old enough to be my father."

The men resumed their fretful trek toward the settlement.

"I wonder if we will be bought up on charges," said one. "I did not come to this land to be put in jail."

"I refuse to go to jail for this," another said grimly. "I will swim back to Spain if I have to."

"It is a long way back," another said gloomily.

"I wish I'd never come on this voyage," said yet another.

"We cannot help it if we are men. God made us this way. He gave us our nature."

So they expected the worst, and some of them stayed away from the settlement where they were likely to run into soldiers.

Several days passed and nothing happened, and every day the men went to the beach where the *Santa Inez* lay on one side in an unladylike pose with her bottom bared to the open skies, and every day they expected trouble from the authorities.

So they waited. And still nothing happened. No one came looking for them. Soldiers passing them in the woodlands paid them no attention. The men did not understand.

Then a few days later an incident occurred in front of them that explained the indifference of the authorities toward the Indians. In full view of several of the crewmen, a soldier grabbed an Indian woman walking past accompanied by a warrior. The woman put up a fight and when the warrior intervened, the soldier drew his sword and hacked both of them to death. Without a backward glance, he sauntered away, leaving the torn and bloody bodies where they had fallen.

As he passed the astonished crew, the soldier rasped angrily, "The heathen scratched me."

It was then clear to the crewmen of the *Santa Inez*: Indians were fair game. Once they had learned this lesson, the crewmen became merciless toward the Arawaks, and if they came across Indian women accompanied by Indian men, they would often kill the warriors before raping the women.

There was no conscience involved: in the eyes of the Spaniards, the Indians were backward, benighted heathens. They were also defenseless. Their weapons of spears tipped with fish bones were useless against Spanish body armor, crossbows, harquebuses, and cannons.

Spanish culture, European aggressiveness, and a

pitiless, genocidal Catholicism fell upon the Arawak tribes with a pestilential ferocity.

CHAPTER 15

You do not give up on a god just because he does not do your bidding. If you give a god love and he returns indifference, you do not abandon him. After all, he is the god and you the worshippper, the beggar, the one seeking favors and blessings.

Take the zemi, for example. It did not save Uncle Brayou, no matter how hard Orocobix had prayed and begged for mercy. Yet Orocobix still honored the zemi and cherished it as the treasure of his few possessions. In the bohio of Orocobix, the zemi still occupied a special place of respect and dignity. Every day Orocobix talked to it just as if the zemi had granted all his wishes and showered him with blessings. It did not faze a faithful heart if a god acted inexplicably. To such an ungiving god, the true worshipper continues to show love and devotion.

That was the thinking of Orocobix during the days that followed his expulsion from the vessel belonging to the gods from the sky. These thoughts were heart-felt and sent him back to the ocean front in search of God Carlos.

He went first to the pier, but the vessel was gone. He then roamed the fringes of the settlement, scanning the faces of the Spaniards for God Carlos; he had been doing so all day and at sunset he had a surprise encounter.

Carlos and the boy Pedro were trudging from the *Santa Inez*, which was still being careened, looking for a place to sleep that night. Orocobix was walking with his eyes downcast, peeping furtively at passing Spaniards, but without drawing too close. He knew from hearsay that the gods were capricious and that venturing too near them could provoke a sudden murderous blow. So he kept his distance yet still studied the face of every passing god. He was scuffling past a tree when the boy Pedro recognized him and cried out, "Señor Carlos, it is your Indian."

"No," said Carlos, glancing up, "it is not."

"It is, señor," the boy Pedro insisted.

To prove that the boy was wrong, Carlos snapped his fingers, and the Indian immediately stopped, turned, and looked at them with astonishment. Then he threw himself at the Spaniard's feet.

"God Carlos!" he cried ecstatically.

"See!" the boy Pedro chortled with triumph.

The god and his follower talked in their strange tongues to each other with little understanding. They used hand signals and pantomiming and gestures, and when exasperation set in because they could not understand each other, they both raised their voices and spoke louder. With the boy Pedro watching, Orocobix spoke Taíno to the god, the god replied in Spanish, and both god and his adorer often tripped and stumbled over misunderstood meanings.

Gradually, Orocobix came to understand that the gods' vessel was being repaired and that having no place to sleep, the two gods were spending the night under the sparse shelter of a tree.

Under a tree was no place for gods to sleep, Orocobix protested vigorously. They should, instead, come with him and stay the night at his bohio. Here they could fill their bellies and sleep peacefully in a *hamaca*.

All this Orocobix made the two gods understand, using gestures and repetition. The boy Pedro, having a young brain, grasped most of what the Arawak was saying.

"He invites us to follow him," Pedro said.

Carlos was suspicious. "Well, I have my knife with me. I'll cut his throat if he tries anything."

"I am your servant," Orocobix declared, beckoning the gods to follow.

"Let's go with him," the boy Pedro urged.

And so as night fell over Sevilla la Nueva, the two gods set out cautiously through the woodlands, following a trail known only to the Indian, who occasionally turned to make sure they were still behind him.

"Tell him I have a knife, and if he tries anything, I'll cut his throat," Carlos whispered to Pedro.

"I do not know the words," the boy whispered back.

"I'll cut your throat!" Carlos shouted at the Indian.

"Not much farther," Orocobix replied over his shoulder.

"I'll cut it from ear to ear!" Carlos yelled.

"I do not think you should say such things to one who worships you, señor," the boy said quietly.

"Shut up," Carlos snapped. "You don't know the wickedness of men like I do."

"You will eat shortly," said Orocobix smoothly, taking a guess at what Carlos was saying.

They trudged on through the gathering darkness which was falling and threatening to blot out the trail underfoot. A feeble light dripped from a wrinkled old moon, casting a sickly pallor over the dark woodlands.

"Not much farther, oh gods from the sky," Orocobix said encouragingly over his shoulder.

"Maybe I should just cut his throat now," Carlos muttered.

"Gods do not do such things," the boy Pedro said calmly. "But then, you're no god."

Carlos swatted him on the back of the head.

"That doesn't make you one, either, señor."

After walking for an hour, they arrived at the village, which they could hear from afar long before they saw it. On a night breeze came a faint singing and drumming that sounded at first like the buzz of a distant colony of insects. Orocobix turned and said with a grin, "*Areito!*"

He had forgotten that the shaman had called for an areito tonight—a ceremonial dance and feasting where the old stories of the beginning would be recited, the ancestors honored, and life communally celebrated.

As they drew nearer to the village, the sound they heard on the breeze became a distinct drumbeat pounding out a seductive rhythm, which got louder and louder. Soon, against the backdrop of an endless night, they glimpsed red and yellow flames in the darkness and a plume of smoke unrolling into the heavens.

They emerged from the woodlands into a lit clearing where a throng of naked Arawaks milled and swirled around an enormous bonfire, dancing and writhing to chanting and the rhythm of drums. Scattered over the ground and carefully avoided by the dancing revelers were zemis from different families representing gods and the ancestors. Although the drumming was loud and the chanting hypnotic, the milling crowd was as energetic and as well behaved as a congregation of Western Christians seized by the Holy Spirit.

At the sight of the two gods with Orocobix, the celebrating horde of naked brown Indians fell silent, the drumming abruptly stopped, and, as if grotesquely synchronized, hundreds of heads turned to gape with astonishment at the strangers.

Orocobix stepped in front of the two gods and

cried out, "The gods from the sky have come among us! Let us greet them as honored guests!"

A roar exploded from the crowd and with a crush of footsteps, naked brown bodies surged forward in a gentle wave to engulf the two gods standing with Orocobix. An enormous tangle of hands reached out like tapping tentacles to gently touch the two gods. Many of the tribe had never seen the gods up close before but had only heard about them or glimpsed them in the distance, and even as Carlos shied away and wheeled to face this one and that one, the boy Pedro did not react with fear but returned the gentle touches with a smile. Like a brown sea, the naked bodies rippled and lapped gently against the strangers in an incoming tide that gradually receded, leaving the two gods and Orocobix enisled in an atoll of Arawaks.

The cacique stepped out of the crowd and approached the gods. Scowling, Carlos eyed him warily.

"We welcome you to our village, oh gods from the sky," the cacique said formally, making a little curtsy of respect.

"What's he saying?" Carlos muttered to the boy Pedro.

"I do not know, señor," replied Pedro, "but it is nothing bad."

For a moment all the figures, daubed with a flickering roseate tint by the flames, were frozen like pageantry players in a tableau. Then Carlos raised his right hand and snapped his fingers. Orocobix looked astonished, but he slowly lowered himself into the prostrated position that Carlos had taught him. The cacique was confused and unsure of what to do, but after a moment's hesitation, he also sprawled out like a groveler beside Orocobix at the feet of the gods from the sky. His advisers followed his example as did the watching throng assembled before the huge fire, falling one by one to their knees as if blown low by the wind, until only one man was left standing defiantly among the bent-over bodies. It was Calliou, the hot-blooded elder, and he stood fiercely erect with a contemptuous expression on his face.

"They are not gods," he cried. "They are only foreign men."

"I do not think he believes in you, señor," the boy Pedro whispered.

"I should strike him down," Carlos growled.

"You are no god, señor," said the boy Pedro, "and you have no weapon but your knife."

"Stop saying that! They will hear you."

From his prone position, Orocobix yelled, "They are gods! Calliou, you dishonor us with your disbelief!"

"Get up off the ground," Calliou cried. "You bow low before men."

"Command them to get up," the boy Pedro whispered urgently, "before they do it on their own."

Carlos made the sign for Orocobix to rise, bringing him scrambling to his feet. Everyone else stood up almost at once, and for a long moment, the Indians and the gods looked each other over speculatively with much fidgeting and whispering.

The silence was broken by Orocobix, who called out, "Food! Fish for the gods!"

"Gods do not eat fish," Calliou rasped, "but dogs and men do."

A few chuckles rippled through the crowd, and one or two old women clucked reprovingly at Calliou as the elder shuffled off to his bohio.

"Seat the gods beside me," the young cacique commanded.

"Food, eat," Orocobix said to the two gods, making a gesture with his hand to his mouth. Both gods understood, and being hungry, they willingly followed him through the crowd to the patch of ground where the duho of the cacique was perched. The big god was given the seat as a sign of respect, and the little god was seated right beside him on a woven cotton blanket.

The drumming and chanting resumed and once again the celebrants began gyrating and dancing around the bonfire as the gods, the cacique, and his advisers ate roasted fish.

Carlos was suddenly in a jubilant mood. "I think I was born to be a god," he said, wolfing down his food.

"To believe that still does not make you a god, señor," said the boy Pedro softly.

Carlos swatted him on this side of the head, hard, with the heel of his hand.

The boy touched his head where he had been struck and almost began crying. But he thought that the Indians would not understand a god who cried. So he bit his tongue and pretended that the blow did not hurt while Carlos ate fish and stared lustily at several naked women who sat nearby whispering and giggling at them.

"God Carlos," Orocobix murmured prayerfully, his eyes brimming with love and devotion.

The night passed quickly, the gods patiently listening and watching as the reciters and chanters took turns telling ceremonial stories of creation, of the God Deminen and his three brothers who walked and lived in the sky. And although they watched the proceedings carefully, the visiting gods did not understand that ancient myths and tales were being told and retold, that the names of long-dead ancestors were being chanted in remembrance. Without writing, the Arawaks had no other way to remember their beloved dead or to preserve the ancient explanations of why "the men of the good," which was the meaning of *Taíno*, were marooned on the earth.

Carlos and the boy Pedro dined that night on cassava bread, roasted fish, potatoes, mamey, guava, and anon, all manner of tubers, nuts, and on the flesh of wild birds that flew in such great perfusion that sometimes they appeared to the eye like a passing cloud. They drank a fermented liquid served in polished gourds and watched as the revelers took turns giving thanks to Yocahu for the bounty of the earth and the sea. To this greatest of gods were offered servings of manioc bread and drink, and his praises were joyfully sung.

The celebration came and went in receding waves of chanting and drumming broken by stretches of silence as the surfeited celebrants either passed out on the ground or staggered off to their bohios or sprawled around the fire staring at nothing. Soon, all that remained behind was the litter of sleeping naked brown bodies scattered around the clearing and the glowing heart of what had been the bonfire.

Carlos and boy Pedro spent the night in Orocobix's bohio, which was made of the trunk and thatch of a single palm tree lashed together in a circular pattern. Inside was cool and dry but bare, being hung with two hammocks, which neither of the gods had ever seen before. There was no armoire, no vanity table or dresser filled with clothing and jewelry, only the faithless zemi propped up against the thatched wall.

Orocobix demonstrated to the two gods how they should climb into the hammocks and sleep, and once Carlos and the boy had settled down, he went outside the bohio and lay across its small open entrance where he spent the night to ensure that no curiosity seeker would disturb his guests.

It was an unnecessary precaution: crime was almost unknown among the Arawaks. No one in a village wanted for anything. No one ever went hungry unless all went hungry. No one possessed anything that anyone else would crave. The nakedness of the people was a reflection of the sparseness and simplicity of their hearts.

The land of the Arawaks was a mild land of plenty with no dramatic change of seasons, no harsh winters, no recurring climactic catastrophes other than the occasional hurricane. In this gentle land the Arawaks went about in their bare skin painted with dye made from the roots of plants.

The Arawaks could have made and worn clothes if they had desired, for even in 1520 Xaymaca was renowned throughout the neighboring islands as a prolific producer of cotton, which the women spent much of their time spinning and weaving. Later, the Spaniards would use Jamaica as the source of sail cloth.

So Carlos and the boy Pedro passed a peaceful night in the bohio while their Indian host slept sprawled across the small doorway like a faithful guard dog.

All this took place during a waning moon that dusted the village and its rows of rounded bohios with a grainy light that resembled a faint yellow pollen. Arawak legends call it "the old man's moon" and say that it is a moon of impending change.

CHAPTER 16

The next morning two women appeared in the doorway of Orocobix's bohio. Both cradled in their arms sick babies. One infant had a roasting fever; the other was wracked with coughing spasms so violent that it seemed on the verge of exploding.

"The gods are still asleep," protested Orocobix.

The women began to make a fuss and raise their voices so that the gods would hear them and wake up, and no matter how hard Orocobix begged them to be quiet, they would not stop.

Hearing the commotion, Carlos and the boy Pedro climbed sleepily down from the hammocks. For a horrible moment neither one of them knew where he was, and they stared at each other with the bewilderment of actors who had blundered into the wrong play. Then the noise from the open doorway recalled them to their circumstances as the world reassembled itself from the pieces shattered by sleep.

Carlos stuck his head out the doorway, which brought a renewed wailing of hope and expectation from the grieving women. The boy Pedro also stood in the open doorway, listening.

"God Carlos," Orocobix said apologetically, "these

are new mothers with sick children. They will not go away."

"What did he say?" Carlos asked the boy Pedro.

"I do not know, but it looks like their babies are sick. When you can't cure them, they will know that we're not gods."

Carlos scratched his hairy chest and made a guttural sound of clearing his throat. "Then I'll cure them both," he boasted with a loud belch.

He took a baby from its mother and felt the surge of unnatural heat coursing through its tiny limbs. Hoisting the baby over his head, he pretended to be muttering an incantation. But what he actually said was, "Recover, baby, or I'll break your heathen neck."

With that, he hurled the naked baby high in the air and caught it as it plunged headfirst back to earth. The mother screamed and yanked her baby from the god and stalked away, hurling at Carlos a backward look of disgust.

Carlos reached for the coughing baby, which the nervous mother handed him reluctantly. Grabbing that baby by the ankles, he began swinging it upside down in the long strokes of a pendulum, all the while chanting, "Get better, you little pagan rat, or I'll feed you to the dog that doesn't bark."

After a few lazy swings, the baby stopped coughing and began changing color. Carlos handed the infant back to its perplexed mother.

"What kind of gods are these?" the mother said

to Orocobix as she shuffled away. But she'd gotten no more than a few yards away when she suddenly stopped, turned, and exclaimed with amazement, "My baby has stopped coughing!" She hurried over to Carlos and threw herself at his feet, hugging her baby and moaning, "Thank you, God Carlos!"

"God Carlos," Orocobix breathed devoutly, falling to his knees.

"What did you do?" asked Pedro.

"Who can say?" Carlos shrugged. "I was trying to terrify it so that it would not cough."

The other woman, witnessing the miracle, came running back, still clutching her feverish baby, and cried, "You cured her baby. Why not mine?"

"What did she say?"

"I do not understand the words," the boy replied, "but I think she wants you to also cure her baby."

"Tell her to go away. I have no cure for fever."

Carlos made a gesture at her to leave him alone, but the woman redoubled her cries. Brown faces popped out from the open doorways of the bohios like turtles from their shells to peer at the commotion.

Carlos was on the verge of kicking the wailing woman when he noticed a curious ornament she wore in her nose: it was a pin, yellow and shiny like gold.

He reached over and touched it, murmuring, "What is this, and where did you get it?"

Orocobix stared at the god. The woman hurriedly pulled the pin from her nose and handed it to the god, her hands shaking, blurting out, "Now will you cure my baby?"

"This is gold," Carlos breathed with an expression of rapture.

"How can you tell?" the boy wondered.

"Any fool knows gold," Carlos declared. "And I'm no fool. Ask the woman where she got it."

"I cannot," the boy Pedro said. "I do not know the words."

Carlos worked some hurried mumbo-jumbo over the sick child then sent it away after trying to make its mother understand that it was cured. As soon as she reluctantly left, mumbling discontentedly to herself, he began to question Orocobix about where she could have found the gold.

Orocobix gradually understood. He pointed to the mountains looming in the distance and asked the god if he would like to go there.

"What did he say?" Carlos asked the boy.

The boy said he did not know.

"Of what use are you?" Carlos asked with exasperation. "You don't know gold. You don't understand these Indians. Of what use are you?"

The boy hung his head and said that he did not know.

His eyes burning with greed, Carlos exclaimed, "This is gold, don't you understand? Finding it can change our lives forever!"

"I can take you there, God Carlos," Orocobix repeated.

* * *

Gold: nothing in all of God's creation was to Spanish explorers more precious. Gold was the object of their deepest cravings.

Yet you could not eat gold. You could not feed it to dogs. Cattle would not graze on it. Pigs would scorn it in their slop. Gold was soft like the belly of a matron and could not withstand heavy manual labor like iron. Colombian Indians used it to make fish hooks, ornaments, and hair tweezers. Later, it would be used to fill decayed teeth. But in 1520, the main use for gold was to make jewelry and trinkets.

The Spanish believed that great quantities of gold lay in the mountains of Jamaica. It was a rumor they had picked up from the other islands, and the attempt to find this phantom gold was a direct cause of the enslavement and eventual extermination of the Jamaican and other West Indian Arawaks. Linked to this futile search for gold was the creation of the evil system known as the *encomienda*.

Introduced in 1501 by Nicolas de Ovando during his term as governor of Hispaniola, an encomienda was the grant of a parcel of land along with absolute rights to the landowner to use its Indian residents as a source of free labor. In exchange, the landowners agreed to convert the Indians to Catholicism and thus save their immortal souls from the fires of hell. Instead of worshipping the wooden zemis of their forefathers, the Arawaks would be taught to kneel before Catholic zemis such as crucifixes and figurines of the saints, angels, and the Virgin Mary. It amounted to throne-sanctioned slavery.

Gold mining in those days required the painstaking sifting through of tons of alluvial deposits in the mountainous areas of the interior. Getting to these deposits meant slogging through dense forests and swamps, braving the heat and mosquitoes and attack by hostile tribes.

The method of mining the gold was crude and labor-intensive. Holes dug into the banks of a fast-flowing section of the river gradually accumulated deposits of dirt and sand, which were carefully sifted through for gold. It was exhausting drudgery that yielded specks of the valuable metal per day and often nothing at all for hours.

In some islands—Hispaniola, for example—this technique, although crude and backbreaking, did result in significant finds of gold. But Jamaica had no gold—not in the interior, not in the foothills, not on the coastline. What Carlos had seen in the woman's nose was an ornamental pin made of *guanin*, an alloy of copper and gold. It was not real gold.

But believing that gold lay strewn over the mountains like wild fruit falling from a government tree, Carlos was plotting to find some and smuggle it back to Spain. If he was successful, he would never be a poor man again. And the truth was that he was sick and weary of being poor and ignored like a stray animal. He hungered for respect, recognition, comfort—all the accoutrements that went with being rich. He wanted what de la Serena had but did not appreciate.

Carlos vowed that once he had the gold, he would not be cynical and indifferent to it like the old man was. He would attend Mass every day. He would make novenas, give money to the poor. He would stop pretending to be God, for he would be rich, and being rich was better than being God.

Carlos had not meant to stay longer than overnight in the Arawak village. But as soon as the women had left, Orocobix served the gods drink and fruit with an expression of devoutness that Carlos, in his vanity, could not resist.

"Already it is hot, God Carlos," said Orocobix apologetically, "but the bohio is cool and comfortable."

God Carlos did not understand. Neither he nor Pedro knew the time but the sun told them that they would have to hurry back to help with the careening.

Since they had slept in their clothes and lived in a time before dental hygiene was a daily ritual, it remained only for Carlos to strap the scabbard in which he kept his dagger around his right ankle and they were ready to return to the beached ship.

That one night at the village was all Carlos and the boy Pedro expected. But at the end of another long day of careening the Santa Inez, the two were walking off the beach with the other men when Orocobix glided out of the bush where he had been waiting all day.

"God Carlos!" he called out. The other men heard and looked knowingly from one to the other, but no one spoke a word within earshot of Carlos about the bizarre name the Indian was calling him.

And so Carlos and the boy Pedro went over to Orocobix and ended up passing another night in the village.

On this second night there was no areito—no communal celebration in which the whole tribe participated. Many of the bohios had open fires just outside their doorways around which families of Indians gathered talking among themselves or playing with their barkless dogs. There were sounds of laughter and a low background babble of soft, intermittent chit-chat that people all over the world use at the end of the day, and every now and again the wail of a hungry baby would pierce the blanket of darkness whose immensity was riddled by pinholes of light made by the scattered open fires, and a mother would dart into a thatched hut to feed her infant.

Some of the Indians curled up and dozed around the dancing sprigs of fire, occasionally stirring to take part in the chatter. There were no guards or sentries posted, and if the night occasionally crackled with an unrecognized sound, as all nights will do, here or there a man might sit up and look around or even pad to the edge of light and peer briefly into the darkness before returning to the fire. They behaved like a people without enemies.

That second night Carlos brought with him a crossbow from the bowels of the ship, for his was an untrusting heart. Using a hand crank, he armed the crossbow with an iron bolt and carried three spares with him.

Carlos and the boy Pedro sat outside the open doorway of Orocobix's bohio, having eaten their fill of cassava, fruit, and roasted fish. The village around them seemed to be floating on the smoky darkness, the individual thatched huts resembling a fleet of ships.

Sometimes an Indian would wander over to the fire and squat next to the gods and say a few words to them. It became evident to the Indians that the older god was not as friendly as the younger one, and many soon learned to leave Carlos in peace and say nothing to him except a cordial greeting.

In the dimness of the night, Carlos and the boy could make out the shape of the village, which was circular, with bigger rectangular bohios in the middle—where the cacique and his kinsmen lived—surrounded by smaller rounded ones occupied by ordinary people. By daylight, the gods could see the design of the village, the small stream that ran nearby, the neat gardens—*conucos*—that were planted with cassava, garlic, potatoes, yautias, and mamey. They discovered that part of the Indian village was staked off as a playing field called a *batey*, where a ceremonial game was played with a rubber ball. Carlos and the boy had never seen rubber before, for it was a material unknown to the Spaniards, and they marveled over it.

They stayed a third night and a fourth, and soon they were sleeping every night in a hammock. Carlos was content. Everywhere he went throughout the village he was greeted with reverence. Indians bowed their heads as he walked past as if he were royalty. Whatever he desired from them was granted immediately. True, he could only make himself and his wishes crudely understood. But even this difficulty made him appear more truly godlike. For as he told Pedro boastfully, which god has ever been completely understood by his worshippers?

"You are not a god, señor."

"Shut up!" Carlos barked. "Your mouth spoils everything."

Now that he was an acknowledged god, Carlos took a new woman every day. Some lay with him willingly, being young and venturesome and curious to know what it was like to be penetrated by a god. Most of the women he took on an impulse, meeting them on the footpath that led to Santa Gloria Bay where the Arawaks beached their canoes. The mood would suddenly come over him, and he would walk boldly up to the woman and rub her pubis and let it be known what he desired.

Some terrified women would flee, dropping behind whatever fruit or gourd filled with fish they were carrying. Carlos would give chase through the woods. For such an ungainly man, he had a surprising quickness and Pedro would hear the woman shrieking and see the bushes spasm where he took her. Sometimes he would not give chase but would simply wait for another woman to appear.

Whatever Carlos did to the women, with their consent or not, it did not take long. The boy Pedro was curious and many times felt the urge to ask Carlos what he did and how he did it. Based on snatches of talk he had overheard from other men combined with what he had imagined, Pedro had a vague idea. But he longed for someone to tell him what was true and what was false. Yet he never asked Carlos.

Several times the boy would stalk close and hide behind a tree to watch, but all he saw was the naked rump of Carlos pumping up and down violently while almost hidden underneath him wriggled the woman, pinned by his bulk, her arms flailing the air helplessly. One time he saw another woman smothered under his bulk but whose hands clasped his naked cheeks as if to help him with the pumping.

Lately, Carlos had been spending hours talking wildly about what he would do when the gold he intended to find had made him rich.

The boy was a good listener and he would hear out the braggadocio plans without interruption or discouragement or contradiction, although he would

sometimes accurately point out to Carlos that last
night he had bought an estate in Cordoba and therefore tonight did not need another in Sevilla. Carlos
would stand corrected and admit his mistake unless
he had been smoking cohiba by inhaling it through his
nose from the y-shaped pipe known as tabaco. Then
his disposition was likely to be contrary and he would
insist on buying castles and estates that were hope-
lessly close to each other, regardless of the enormous expense. If he had taken snuff made of seeds
of *anadenanthera peregrina*, which the Arawaks used as
a hallucinogen, he would become openly belligerent
and buy recklessly without regard to reason or econo-
my. At such times, the boy Pedro had learned to leave
him alone to spend his imaginary gold as wantonly as
he pleased.

Sometimes when he had used the snuff, Carlos
would fall into a quarrelsome mood and become aggressive and pick fights. In one such fight, he killed
a warrior right in front of the man's family, drawing
the dagger from his ankle sheath and plunging it into
the man's eye. Orocobix, who had tried his best to
break up the fight, witnessed the ugly scene. Afterward, Carlos was testy and surly and appeared ready
to kill again until the hallucinogen had worn off and
his sanity returned.

In these early days of his godhood, Carlos grew
puffed up with pride and self-importance. Women
still came to him for help—even though the fever-

ish baby had died the day after he'd proclaimed it cured—and the village as a whole seemed content and boastful that not only was the god from the sky their friend, he also slept among them.

Carlos, who had the build of a warthog, began to strut like a peacock. Pride and arrogance oozed out of every porcine pore. The more women he lay with, the more inflated he became, swelling visibly on his own estimation. And always there was a chatter about finding gold and becoming rich and the dreams of how he would live the rest of his life as a man of wealth.

One evening he attacked a pretty Indian woman in the woods, beat her for resistance, and raped her repeatedly. She was the daughter of the elder, Calliou.

CHAPTER 17

"This Carlos is not a god nor a man," said Calliou bitterly. "He is a beast."

Orocobix stirred restlessly. He was sitting cross-legged outside his bohio in the glow of a small fire with Calliou and his daughter Colibri, whose name meant hummingbird, her face still bruised and swollen from the beating Carlos had given her during the rape.

"He is no god," she said in a sullen voice, barely able to speak because her lips were so swollen. "I have taken men inside me before. This was a man."

Calliou winced at such frankness from his daughter. He rubbed the dirt with his naked feet and stared around him at the slumbering village.

It was well past midnight, and the moonless night was cooled by a breeze scented with rain. The village was girthed by a belt of darkness so immense and deep that the three people sitting before the embers of a dying fire might have thought themselves abandoned castaways. Fifty yards away, in Orocobix's bohio, slept Carlos.

"The beast should die for what he did to my daughter," Calliou said angrily.

"He is a god," Orocobix said. "He cannot die."

Colibri shifted on the dirt and looked up at the stars. "If he is a god . . ." she said thoughtfully.

"He is," insisted Orocobix.

"Then he will not die even if he is killed," she murmured.

No one spoke for a long time, and the silence was broken by the whistling of tree frogs and the sinister rattling of croaking lizards.

"He wishes to go where gold is found," Orocobix said, after another long stretch of silence.

No one said a word; no one moved, not even when an alco slunk past the sputtering fire and was swallowed whole by the yawning mouth of darkness.

In 1520 death was a presence that frequented every corner of life and walked everywhere that men did. People died suddenly, often young, and of ailments that no longer kill. Smallpox, for example, was a global wholesaler of death. Today it is a lame peddler that hobbles door-to-door retailing death to a few remote villages in the undeveloped world.

So it was no surprise to the hardened crew of the *Santa Inez* when some among them began to die. The first to die was the grommet Alonzo, a boy of unknown age—possibly thirteen—who succumbed to the fever. He died aboard ship crying for the mother he never knew, for he was a foundling who had been raised by unloving nuns. He died in spite of being bled three times at the expense of de la Serena.

The next day, the *Santa Inez*, manned by a skeleton crew of eight, barely enough to handle the ship, set out with Monsieur for a mapping sail around the island. Her bilge had been scraped clean, her old ballast of European stones that had grown foul and smelly with moss and mold thrown out and replaced by new stones found on the banks of a nearby river. Once emptied of ballast, her bilge was sprinkled with vinegar. With her armpits freshened and her ballast changed, the *Santa Inez* smelled unnaturally sweet, like a recently bathed whore.

She left at dawn in a light land breeze blowing off the mountains steadily enough to ghost her out of the bay and around the edge of the reef. Before she cleared the reef, the small body of the dead boy, wrapped in sailcloth and weighted down with river stones, was cast into the sea without ceremony.

"Look here!" de la Serena screamed at the men. "You should have waited for deep water!"

"He was beginning to stink," one of the men cried.

"Look sharp now!" de la Serena bellowed. "Watch for shoals."

Because the island had not yet been charted, the *Santa Inez* had to tap her way with a sounding line through unmarked shoals that mottled the clear water like dark sores. Once clear of the shallows she found blue water, caught a northeast quartering wind, and loped west with the serrated coastline off her port beam.

She sailed without Carlos and the boy Pedro. The boy had just weathered a bout of belly sickness. Carlos was afire with gold fever. Moreover, he thought that now was the time, with most of the crew gone, to comb the hills for the gold that he hoped would make him rich. He forced Pedro to come along because his young brain better understood the Taíno language than Carlos did.

As the *Santa Inez* nudged her nose around the edge of the reef and lay a course toward Negril Point, the two gods and Orocobix set out for the mountainous bosom of the island.

On the outskirts of the village, they were joined by Calliou.

"Why is he coming too?" the boy Pedro wondered.

Orocobix indicated with gestures that Calliou knew the place of gold well and would be useful.

"I do not think he should come," Pedro said to Carlos.

Carlos scanned the naked Indian. He had no weapon; he wore no clothing where one might be hidden. Carlos, on the other hand, had with him a loaded crossbow from the ship's armory with four additional bolts. His dagger was sheathed in his ankle scabbard. He also wore a cuirass—chest armor—even though it was heavy and oppressively hot. He took the boy's advice as a dare rather than a warning. His contemptuous glance said that he was more than a match for twenty Indians.

"He can come," Carlos said, "but if he ever stands right behind me, I will cut his throat."

Once the wishes of God Carlos were made known to the two Indians, the four set out in single file on a thin trail through the undergrowth and toward the looming mountains, which looked deceptively close. After slogging through the thicket for hours, they seemed to draw no closer to the mountains. Weighed down by the heavy cuirass, Carlos stopped frequently to rest. The two Indians and the boy would sit and dally in the shade while Carlos blew hard like an over-worked mule.

"How much farther?" Carlos asked querulously, pointing to the mountain and to the small twig of gold the grateful mother had given him.

Orocobix understood. "It is close, God Carlos," he said soothingly.

"What did he say?" Carlos asked Pedro.

The boy shrugged and guessed that it was no more than what the Indian had already said—that the gold was not far away.

"I'll cut your damn throat if you don't stop staring at me," Carlos growled at Calliou, who looked quickly away.

"I think we should turn back," the boy Pedro urged.

"Why?"

"Because I do not like the way they're whispering."

"Let them whisper. I'll kill the first one who looks

at me again," and Carlos drew his finger across his throat.

With that threat in the air, the god lumbered to his feet and the men and boy resumed their journey.

It was hot that day in 1520. The month was October, the end of the hurricane season then and now. In the afternoon of this particular day a feverish stillness had seized the land as the heat mauled both living and dead without mercy.

It was too hot to talk, so they walked without talking. It was too hot to walk, so they stopped often to rest in the shade of majestic trees that grew all over the island—mahogany, royal palm, cotton, and flame heart. Massive flocks of birds passed overhead, dragging the woodlands with enormous shadows like wavering fishnets.

As they walked deeper into the woodlands, the boy Pedro became even more fearful and kept looking over his shoulder.

"Someone is following us," he whispered to Carlos.

Carlos stopped and took a long look through the leaves and bramble. The two Indians also stopped and peered curiously at the gods.

"There's no one there," Carlos said gruffly.

"I tell you I heard something," the boy insisted.

"It is your imagination," Carlos scoffed, indicating to the Indians that they should continue.

The trail had been tamped down by the accumulated footsteps over the years but was so narrow that the three men and the one boy were scratched repeatedly by the overhang of bushes and trees.

Eventually, weary and sweaty, they came to a shiny river unreeling an endless tongue through the throat of a gorge. The two Indians immediately plunged into the water with joyful whoops and were soon splashing and ducking one another like exuberant children. Pedro joined them and also began frolicking in the cool water.

Suddenly the boy stood up and pointed, crying to Carlos, "There's someone hiding behind that tree!"

Carlos turned quickly to look but saw nothing except the woodlands veiled like a penitent by the shadows.

"Are you going mad?" he asked the boy crossly.

Carefully setting on the ground his loaded crossbow and his deerskin shoes, Carlos put his right big toe into the cool river and waded in cautiously, almost distastefully, for he was a man who heartily disliked being wet. Grimacing, he stepped gingerly into the water and felt the current coiling around his ankles like a noose.

The river looked shallow, but its sandy bed was uneven, rocky, and hollowed out with holes marked only by stiller, shinier patches of water. The Indians knew where these were and avoided them, but Carlos did not see them in the placidity of the moving river because he was in the middle of a vivid daydream

about how rich he was about to become and how
he would relish all the treasures that wealth would
bring—respect, comfort, love, attention, servants,
and fine clothes.

Caught up in this fantasy he stepped suddenly
into a hole in the riverbed and, weighed down by
the cuirass which gripped his chest in an iron fist, he
plunged like a dagger into the river's heart.

The boy Pedro saw and cried, "Carlos!"

The two Indians splashed over to where the god
had disappeared. Looking down, they saw him claw-
ing desperately at the water and gaping up at them
with terror.

Between them a dark thought darted like a foraging bat. Neither one moved. They simply peered down
stonily as Carlos, pinned to the bottom of the hole by
the body armor, waved frantically for help.

"Help him!" the boy Pedro screamed, rushing toward them. "He's drowning!"

Calliou blocked his way. "If he is a god, he cannot
die," he said gruffly, holding back the boy.

As they watched, Carlos struggled to tear off the
cuirass, which held him on the sandy bottom of the
river in a death-grip of weight that all his furious
wriggling could not loosen. His eyes screaming for
help, Carlos exploded in a frenzy of movement, wildly
flailing his arms. Pedro's screams rolled through the
river gorge in a deafening volley.

The short and furious fight ended abruptly as Carlos drowned: his wriggling dwindled into uncoordinated spasms; his bursting lungs, filling with water, surrendered the last pocket of precious breath in a spiraling coil of bubbles. Carlos went limp in the murderous embrace of his own body armor, his starkly staring eyes gaping with silent terror. His body slumped over and sank deep in the hole where it remained upright like an underwater stump. The two Indians watched him attentively to be sure that he was dead. Then they pulled him up and wedged his waterlogged body between two rocks.

Staggering out of the river, the Indians collapsed wearily on the bank, panting for air.

"You murdered him," the boy howled.

"Don't cry, young god," Orocobix said soothingly to the sobbing boy, "for he will come back."

Colibri drained out of the dark woods and cautiously waded into the river to peer at the dead body crumpled white and puffy between the rocks like a giant waterlogged slug. She poked at it repeatedly with a stick to be sure it was dead.

With a shriek, Pedro ran away in the direction from which they had come. Calliou leaped to his feet to give chase.

"Let him go," Orocobix said. "He has hurt no one."

The afternoon faded into evening and the dust of nightfall gathered over the gorge. On the riverbank, the three Indians sat together, their toes tingling in the sliding sheet of water.

God Carlos, wedged between the rocks, was beginning to bloat as his lifeless body occasionally twitched to the tug of the current, and his gaping, sightless eyes stared at the gorge with the stern fixity of a public statue.

"Any moment now, he will regain life," Orocobix said repeatedly as their wait first began. But as the afternoon crested into evening, he said it less and less often. By the time dusk was furrowing like a darkening brow, he was silent.

The first time he said it, Calliou grated, "If he comes to life, I'll hit him with a rock."

"No!" Orocobix had replied sharply. "We kill him only once."

"It is enough to do only once," agreed Colibri.

"It is enough," conceded her father.

"Any moment now, and he will return," Orocobix whispered.

A darkness without mercy settled over the gorge.

"It grows dark," Colibri murmured.

"It is nothing," said Orocobix. "Darkness does not hurt."

The others didn't reply. Calliou grabbed his legs and pulled them against his chest as a chill from the river seeped through the gorge and into his bones.

"He will come back," Orocobix said. "Any moment now. You will see."

CHAPTER 18

They slept on the bank of the river close to where the body of Carlos was wedged between the rocks, and on this moonless night the dead Spaniard seemed to blossom in a pouch of whiteness like a night-blooming flower. They talked about whether they should stay awake to see if Carlos would return, but Calliou said that there was no need since the man from the sky was not only clearly a man but one who was also dead. Orocobix disputed this and vowed to stay awake to greet the risen Carlos.

And at first, Orocobix did stay awake. But the sounds made by the river were so soothing that he eventually fell asleep along with the others. When he woke up dawn was breaking and the river humming contentedly to itself as it fed on the gorge.

Leaping to his feet, he rushed to the water's edge and looked for the body. It was gone. All he could see was the river sliding through the gorge in a continuous tongue of shiny water. But there was no sign of the body.

"He has risen!" Orocobix cried triumphantly, awakening his two companions.

Calliou and Colibri did not believe even after they

were fully awake and standing beside Orocobix and carefully scanning the empty river. They still did not believe even after they waded into the river out to the rocks where they had left the body and saw for themselves that it was gone. All they saw shining in the bottom of the hole was the cuirass lying on its side like a dead fish. Even then they did not believe.

Calliou splashed downstream, searching among the fringe of water plants and reeds lining the riverbanks but could find no trace of the body. The more the three Indians looked the more jubilant Orocobix became. He was convinced that Carlos had come back to life while the three of them slept and was vexed with himself for not staying up to greet him.

"I'm sorry, God Carlos," he kept muttering like one possessed.

"We will find it if we look long enough," Colibri declared as they waded downstream combing the banks.

But they did not find it even after walking until they came to where the sluggish river was shattered into an eddying cataract by the steep drop of a waterfall. If the body had drifted downstream it would not have cleared this part of the river where the water was a shimmering slice rolling taut and thin over sheer rock. And if it had miraculously come this far, the body should be trapped in the foaming cataracts at the foot of the falls.

But they saw no sign of a body. They saw no scraps of clothing that Carlos wore. A quarrelsome mood broke out among them. In his heart Orocobix fervently believed that God Carlos had risen and walked away from the gorge. Calliou and Colibri were just as adamant that some physical explanation was behind the disappearance of the body.

After some discussion, the three Indians decided to return to the village. They saw no reason to remain here, for there was no body. Calliou thought to dive down and retrieve the peculiar garment that the God Carlos had been wearing when he drowned, and several times he battled the current of the river and tried to lift up the cuirass lying at the bottom of the hole, but he did not have the strength or the breath, and when he asked Orocobix to help, the other said no, that he would not retrieve anything that might be used to prove that Carlos was not a God. And so they squabbled on the riverbank but the cuirass was not brought up and eventually they set off for the village.

They trudged in silence through the thicket of the woodland following the trail that marked the land like the scar of an old wound. Orocobix tried his best not to gloat. They were almost to the village when Colibri wondered, "What will we tell the cacique?"

"We can only tell him what we saw," Calliou said gruffly, "for anything we say, Orocobix will say something different."

"I will tell only the truth," said Orocobix.

"There is no truth," Colibri countered. "There is only explanation."

* * *

What had happened to God Carlos?

A crocodile had taken him. During the night the hunting beast had detected the putrefying carcass and glided over and seized it by the leg. It had dragged the body upriver and stored it in a hole in the riverbank where in the underwater murkiness it would snack piecemeal on it over the next two weeks, for the beast liked flesh that was rotting.

Between the Arawaks and crocodiles there was no love and little contact. None of the middens left behind by the extinct Indians contains any trace of crocodile bones, an absence that would in our own time mystify paleontologists. But its explanation is simple: the Arawak weapons were too puny to kill crocodiles. Moreover, the Indians found the beast so fearsome that they avoided its haunts.

While the three Indians were searching for dead Carlos, the body was snug in the underwater pantry of an ancient reptile that was breeding a clutch of eggs with a surprising gentleness. And every now and again, like an ugly, translucent shadow, the creature would glide out of the hole in which it lived to tear off another chunk of flesh from the dead Spaniard.

God Carlos was no communion Eucharist that the monster ate for the sake of its soul, for it was impossible to imagine that there could be a spiritual half to such a grotesquerie. To the soulless beast, God Carlos was nothing more than food.

* * *

What was he to do?

That was the question that tormented the boy Pedro as he fled through the woodlands toward the settlement. Most of the time he ran, but occasionally when he was breathless, he would stop and rest against a tree and listen for the footsteps of a pursuer. But he heard nothing. The woodland was a frightening place of thick shadows and suspicious sounds and he did not stop long in it, for whenever he did he felt a touch of raw fear.

Over and over again he relived the drowning and saw the Indians looking on stonily as it happened. Pedro had not particularly liked Carlos, but he was only a boy and had spent many hours in the company of the older man. Carlos had never treated him kindly, but neither had he ignored him as the other crew members did. He had been to the older man like a tolerated dog, and though Carlos often cuffed him on the side of the head for capricious reasons, even such rough treatment was better than being ignored.

What puzzled the boy was why the Indians had allowed Carlos to drown. He thought the act had something to do with the woman Carlos had dragged screaming off the trail and into the woods a few days ago. What he had done to her in the woods the boy Pedro still did not entirely know. But somehow that deed was responsible. He did not know that the woman was named Colibri and that her father was Calliou.

As for the indifference of Orocobix during the drowning of his god, what explanation could anyone give as to why he had done nothing to help save Carlos? His behavior made no sense to the boy.

Deep in thought, he came to the outskirts of the village where Arawak women were busy planting by walking in a line across a field and using sticks to bore holes in the soil into which they dropped seeds. All of them knew the young god by sight, and many glanced up and greeted him as he walked past looking at no one, his heart torn by the drowning of Carlos.

He disappeared into the woods, with the cries of, "Young God! Young God!" from Arawak women ringing in the air. He reached the settlement that evening, still undecided about what to do, when he ran into old Hernandez.

He found the old man resting against the trunk of a tree. The time ashore had made him ragged and disheveled, for since the ship had sailed, he had been living outdoors and eating very little. Yet his mood was not downcast. He had an old man's view of life and knew there was no point in either extreme jubilation or dejection, for neither feeling was lasting. The church preached this doctrine of temporariness, and to this day it is the underpinning of the serious religious temperament. But a long full life that made him witness to the inevitability of change, not any proclamation by the pope, had brought old Hernandez to this period of steadiness.

After sharing some pieces of bread with the old man, the boy Pedro told his gruesome story with much weeping and gory detail. The old man listened calmly, and at the end of the story, he stared long and hard at the sky like one reading omens from the pattern of clouds.

"I do not know what to do," sobbed Pedro.

"Nothing is the best thing to do if you're unsure about what to do," mumbled the old man.

"They let him drown."

"But they did not hurt you," observed old Hernandez. "And after he drowned, they sat on the banks of the river and waited. Why? What were they waiting for?"

"I do not know the why or the what, señor," blurted the boy. "I only know what they did. I do not know their reason for doing it."

The two sat silent, deep in thought, and then the old man stirred, for he had a sudden idea.

"Could it be that they were trying to prove that he was a god?"

The boy was struck by this idea. He sat up and stared at the old man with undisguised wonder. "It must be," he said in a hushed voice. "That is it, of course."

"Allowing Carlos to drown was a test of faith, then," old Hernandez said without irony, "like saying a Mass for a soul in Purgatory."

After a long pause for reflection, the boy Pedro

asked, "So what should I do? What should I say if anyone asks me about Carlos?"

"You should do nothing, and say nothing. No one
will care. He is not a soul that the world will miss."

"Señor de la Serena is sure to ask about him."

"Then you must tell a lie, for if the soldiers find
out what happened, they will slaughter the Indians."

"I do not like to tell lies, señor. It is a sin that can
land you in hell."

"We are already in hell," old Hernandez responded.

The boy Pedro did not understand, for although
his brain was young and fresh, he had lived only a
dozen or so years of life and had only begun to learn
of the world's wickedness.

"The Indians are a doomed people," old Hernandez said. "It's too bad that Carlos wasn't a real god,
for perhaps he could have saved them."

"He wouldn't have," Pedro said bitterly. "He
would've made them do tricks like dogs. He would've
tormented them."

"That is how gods are," murmured old Hernandez. "They are fickle. They like to tease."

They were silent for a little while, each consumed
with his own thoughts.

The boy gazed out at his surroundings: before his
eyes in the golden glow of the sunset lay a land of un-
matched loveliness. He beheld rolling hills bedecked
in a shade of lush green that his eyes had rarely seen
in desiccated old Europe. His eyes were treated to an

ocean whose clarity and shimmering tones of blue and green would make the celebrated seas of the Old World seem like yesterday's watery porridge. Beyond the slope of the hills he saw white sand beaches grinning endlessly at the heavens as if the small waves that lapped the shoreline were ticklish.

And though he looked, the boy didn't really take in any of this beauty. He had the mind of a child which could cope but had not yet learned to marvel. His eyes had feasted on the pestilential cities of slummy old Europe and were unused to seeing the land naked as its people, adorned only in the contours and colors of God's handiwork. He did not see beauty; he saw only emptiness and desolation.

"I want to go home," he said. "I want to leave this place."

"You are an orphan," replied old Hernandez in a gruff but not unkindly voice. "Everywhere is home to the orphan."

"I do not like this place."

"It is the time you do not like, not the place. Men always mix them up."

The boy Pedro settled down on the bare earth. Night had fallen. He did not understand the riddles in which old Hernandez spoke. There was no moon. There was only darkness and the overhead glistening immensities of starlight. He did not like when there were so many stars that no hand or mind could count them.

* * *

Everything has a beginning, a middle, and an end. It is no different with a voyage. Usually there is a specific commercial purpose behind a voyage—transporting men or goods to a distant land where they are needed—that will provide these stages. But the *Santa Inez* was in the New World for reasons of personal vanity—a rich old man desired a memorial in the newly discovered land. When its journey would be finished depended on one man's whim not on the accomplishment of a shared task that all could see and measure. So no one knew when she would leave, and all the crew from old Hernandez to the boy Pedro felt as if they were wedged in a crack of time.

When Pedro woke up the next morning, none of this was on his mind. Stark memories of his friend being drowned still haunted him. Instead of waking up gradually and peacefully, he bolted upright off the ground and burst into consciousness with a violent start. He found himself under a tree. Nearby old Hernandez slept curled up near the trunk.

The boy was sore because the patch of ground that had been his bed was hard and rocky, and he had tossed fitfully for most of the night. It was only sunrise but already he was sweaty.

He wondered where the ship was and scanned the empty sea for a sail. He saw none. All he saw was a vast and crinkly spectacle of blue water stretching to the horizon that arced against the skyline like a drawn bow.

Old Hernandez woke up and looked at the boy.

"No sign of the ship," Pedro said gloomily.

Old Hernandez rubbed his eyes and coughed. He curled up again on the ground and fell back asleep.

It was Sunday, October 7, 1520. The *Santa Inez* had been in Jamaica now for over six months.

CHAPTER 19

The *Santa Inez* poked her way around Jamaica so the French cartographer, Monsieur, could make a sketch of the island's shape. What would come of the voyage would be a blobby map that made Jamaica look like an amoeba, an organism invisible to the world until 1673 when Anton van Leeuwenhoek of Holland built the first microscope. In reality the island is tapered and symmetrical like a capsule—another invention that was several hundred years away—and does not at all look like the early attempts at mapping it.

During the expedition the Frenchman was cheerful company for de la Serena, and they spent many hours on the night sea discussing the meaning of life and what would happen after death.

What was wrong with oblivion? de la Serena asked the Frenchman often. Why did men fear it when it was nothing fearful? You had no consciousness. You had no memory. You had no fears. You had the unfeeling placidity of stone. No one had ever seen stone tossing and turning in a sleepless night. Stone did not fret about money. It did not have plots and ambitions that might come to nothing. What was so wrong with being stone?

Monsieur knew immediately what was wrong with oblivion. There was no food in oblivion—no sauces, no sausages, no soufflés. A man who loved his belly as much as Monsieur did found the idea of oblivion gastronomically revolting.

So the argument went back and forth, sometimes late into the night when the *Santa Inez* would heave to in a land breeze, her head bobbing up and down like a trotting donkey.

Circumnavigating Jamaica, which would ordinarily take a vessel like the *Santa Inez* barely a day, consumed almost a week because she kept circling the island to give Monsieur ample opportunity to perfect his map.

As he drew the map, Monsieur lavishly proposed naming different notable features of the island after de la Serena. He threw the older man several bones— proposing to name the westernmost point of the island Point de la Serena instead of Negril Point. He did the same for Morant Point, the Blue Mountains, and Lovers' Leap, until even de la Serena realized that his name could not be on every geographic feature and, after some bargaining, settled for the island's most prominent feature—the Blue Mountains.

On his map of Jamaica in 1520, Monsieur named this rugged mountain that crowns the island with a massive monarchial presence Mount de la Serena. When the Spaniard saw by flickering candlelight his name scribbled on the parchment above this massive

bulk, he shook with a tremor of happiness and felt
that the long voyage of the *Santa Inez* had been more
than repaid. He had his memorial. Now he could go
home.

On her third turn around the island, off the south
side near the stretch of coastline known on maps
today as Alligator Reef, the *Santa Inez* encountered a
large canoe filled with many Indians. She drew near
to investigate when an Arawak guide who had briefly
gone below, appeared on deck with a warning cry. De
la Serena and Monsieur were trying to understand
what the Indian was shrieking about when a volley of
arrows flew out of the canoe and peppered the deck of
the ship. One arrow grazed the shoulder of Monsieur.
By the time the undermanned crew ran out the guns
of the *Santa Inez*, the canoe had scuttled toward the
shoreline in an area too shallow for her to follow, and
the Indians escaped.

"Canaballi! Canaballi!" the Arawak was shouting over and over again, making a movement like one
swooning.

Monsieur sat down on the deck, carefully finger-
ing his wound. The Indian guide, meanwhile, was
babbling loudly and gesturing to make himself understood. Finally, one of the men grasped what he was
saying: the Indians in the canoe were marauding Caribs, cannibals who ate the flesh of their human enemies. Their arrows were tipped with a deadly poison.

Monsieur suddenly felt weak and had trouble

breathing. He collapsed on the deck and began gasping from the effect of *curare*, a poison made from a rainforest vine that causes paralysis and the inability to breathe by blocking the work of neural transmitters.

"What's happening to me?" Monsieur gasped, seizing de la Serena by the arms.

"The Indian says the arrow was poisoned," de la Serena said softly, adding, "but what does an Indian know?"

A hardened look took ahold of Monsieur. "I do not agree to this," he spat fiercely. "I will not die from this. I refuse to die."

The *Santa Inez* set a course for New Seville, her men scanning the sea for more canaballi. She encountered no more canoes, made her way into Santa Gloria Bay without incident, and tied up at the quay as Monsieur lay dying below deck in de la Serena's private quarters.

It was the worst possible thing that could happen from de la Serena's point of view. If Monsieur should die, who would complete the drawing of the map of the island? Who would name the massive mountain Mount de La Serena? Once again his ambition would be thwarted. He was angry and frustrated and spent many hours pacing the quarterdeck and obsessively checking on Monsieur.

De la Serena was, by now, fed up with drab settlement life. Indian women, on whom his crew preyed daily, meant nothing to him—an old man. Living in the New World was little better than living like a range chicken constantly scratching the earth for food. The days were long and boring. Even worse were the nights, which came and went with a depressing sameness. Death was everywhere. He was ready to go home. The voyage of the *Santa Inez* was approaching its end.

During that week, while Monsieur hovered in a coma, de la Serena let it be known that his boat would sail shortly and he became engrossed in the many little details a ship's master must attend to before embarking on a long voyage. Most important of all was to do a head count of the available crew.

It was then that he discovered Carlos was missing.

De la Serena summoned the boy Pedro and asked him what had happened to Carlos. The boy said he was unsure but believed that the man had gone off into the interior of the island with an Indian woman. Other crewmen were asked about the missing sailor, but none could add anything to the boy's story. Finally, beleaguered with preparations for the voyage home, de la Serena gave up inquiring about Carlos and decided to leave well enough alone. The man had been a troublemaker to begin with. No one would miss him. As far as de la Serena was concerned, Carlos had jumped ship.

He scratched off the name of Carlos Antonio Maria Eduardo Garcia de la Cal Fernandez from the ship's roster, a preposterous combination of words that had been signified on the rolls only by the seaman's careful scrawl of his first name on the parchment. It was as if he'd never come to Jamaica, never even been on the *Santa Inez*.

And that was the official end of God Carlos.

One morning some days later, Monsieur awoke from his coma and got up off his deathbed.

The Frenchman's explanation of his recovery was simple enough: he had refused to die. It would be a topic that he and de la Serena would continue debating for the long voyage back to Spain.

The *Santa Inez* had spent approximately six months on the island, and when she sailed early one morning in a brisk land breeze, no official delegation was ashore to see her leave. Of her arriving crew of twenty, she had lost seven, not counting Carlos who was presumed to have jumped ship—six to the fever, and one to Carlos's dagger. Yet when she sailed on October 23, 1520, she had a full complement of men because several soldiers whose military term of commitment had expired signed on as crew. To this number was added a handful of vagabond adventurers who had come to the New World to seek their fortunes and were now returning empty-handed to their grim lives in sixteenth-century Spain. She had arrived unannounced like a thief; she sneaked out like an unwelcome guest. And almost no one cared.

There was one sorrowful witness who grieved to see her leave. It was Orocobix, who had just begun a day of fishing on the deep side of the reef.

He did not know that the *Santa Inez* would sail that morning, for he had avoided her and her crew ever since the drowning. His entire tribe had lived in fear of retribution from the Spaniards and had been steeling themselves for attack. But none came. The days slipped past and every night watchmen posted on the outskirts of the village sounded no alarm. Eventually, the tribe relaxed and the village slipped back into its easygoing daily rhythms.

With the men lounging about on the deck as men will do at the beginning of a long voyage, the caravel slipped through the channel and pointed her nose out to deep sea. The boy Pedro was in the bow, where his friend Carlos used to sit, as the ship sliced her way past the fishing canoe. His mind distracted by a daydream, the boy made eye contact with Orocobix and gave a little gasp of recognition. He stared at the fishing Indian and walked down the length of the deck as if to keep him in sight, but soon he was at the stern of the ship, where de la Serena paced with the Frenchman at his side as they slid past the little canoe and headed out to the deep blue sea unreeling a squiggle of a wake like the broken string of a kite. Then he was standing where he didn't belong, staring silently at the receding canoe.

"There's a story there," chuckled Monsieur to de la Serena, who was frowning at the effrontery of a cabin boy being on this part of the ship without reason.

The moment was broken by the cry of old Hernandez, who was the only other person on the ship to know what was happening, summoning Pedro back to the bow. Orocobix waved, and the boy waved back.

It did not mean much to either one, that wave. It signaled no understanding, no love, not even a once-shared feeling or commonality of purpose. Between them—the boy of Spain and the Indian of the New World—passed nothing deeper or of greater conse-quence than raw recognition. It was no more than stone waving to shell or metal waving to wood, the inanimate to the lifeless. As the vessels separated, the lovely landform that was Jamaica loomed between them like a referee.

CHAPTER 20

History is drama acted out by human beings on a worldwide stage. Most of the drama is inconsequential and repetitious. But some acts and scenes are highly instructive and teach valuable lessons. Often, it is only after the props have been put away and the actors have gone from the stage forever that we begin to glimpse the meaning of a particular act.

By 1520, the Spanish had spread throughout the Caribbean like a virulent pestilence and were slaughtering the defenseless Arawaks. One observer of the Spaniards' viciousness was Bartolome de las Casas, a Catholic priest who served as an adviser to the colonial governor of Santo Domingo. In 1542, in his *Brief Account of the Devastation of the Indies,* he described the brutality and barbarism with which the Arawaks were treated:

> *The Christians, with their horses and swords and pikes, began to carry out massacres and strange cruelties against them [the Arawaks]. They attacked the towns and spared neither the children nor pregnant women and women in childbed, not only stabbing them and dismembering them but cutting them to pieces as if dealing with sheep*

in the slaughterhouse. They laid bets as to who, with one stroke of the sword, could split a man in two or could cut off his head or spill out his entrails with a single stroke of the pike. They took infants from their mothers' breasts, snatching them by the legs and pitching them headfirst against the crags or snatched them by the arms and threw them into the rivers, roaring with laughter and saying as the babies fell into the water, "Boil there, you offspring of the devil!"

Las Casas was writing about what he had witnessed in Santo Domingo, but the same grisly genocidal scenario was played out in Jamaica.

No one knows for certain how many Arawaks were living in Jamaica when Columbus "discovered" the already well-known island in 1494. Some estimates put the population at 50,000; others, at 100,000. What is known is that by 1655 when the English overran Jamaica, the Indians had become extinct. Many would die of infectious diseases spread by the invaders. Others would be slaughtered by the Spaniards in skirmishes and battles. Still others would be sent to dig futilely for gold in the interior of the island and would die from hard labor. In despair over their enslavement, thousands of Arawaks would commit mass suicide by drinking unfermented cassava juice.

Las Casas lived to be ninety-two years old and came to be nicknamed Apostle of the Indians. Through his efforts, the New Laws were enacted in 1542 abolishing the encomienda system and forbidding the use of Arawaks as a source of slave labor. It was too late: the Arawaks were already trudging down the road to extinction.

Las Casas had by then also planted another terrible seed that would grow even more bitter fruit: he had recommended the use of African blacks as a source of labor in place of the Arawaks. Horrible and prolonged would be the nightmare to ensue from a proposal intended innocently as an act of mercy.

There were two distinct peoples thriving in the Caribbean—the Arawaks and the Caribs—when the Spanish first arrived in 1492. A little more than one hundred years later the Arawaks had been exterminated. Today the Caribs, who put up a fierce fight against the invader, still exist. Many Spanish soldiers fell to the poisonous arrows of these canaballi, and soon the invader learned to avoid those islands they were known to occupy. If the drama of the Arawaks teaches anything, it is that passivity in the face of a vicious invader is a bad tactic.

In an ironic twist, the Arawaks got their revenge on the Europeans. In 1494, John de Vigo DeVito wrote this of a strange new disease:

> *In the yeare of our Loard, 1494, in ye monethe of December when Charles ye Frenche kynge toke hys iorney into the partes of Ytaly, to recouer the kyngdome of Naples,*

there appered a certayne dysease through out al Ytaly
of an unknowen nature, whych sondrye nations hath
called by sondry names . . . Thys dysease is contagious,
chiefly yf it chaunce through copulation of a man wyth
an unclene woman, for the begynnynge therof was in the
secret members of men and women . . .

The new disease was syphilis, which was endemic
to the Arawaks and is spread through sexual contact.
The boil on his penis that de Morales spoke of before
his death was the first sign of infection. If Carlos had
not killed de Morales in a knife fight, syphilis would
have done the job or driven him mad. Once transmit-
ted to Europe, it spread throughout the population
and resulted in an untold number of deaths. That was
the legacy, and revenge, of the Arawaks.

More than four hundred years have passed since the
voyage of the *Santa Inez*. She was a brave, stout vessel
and did all that was asked of her by a race of hard,
brutal men.

After the voyage was over and the *Santa Inez* had
returned to Cádiz, she remained tied up at a public
wharf for a year, gradually assuming the frowsy look
of abandonment. Eventually, de la Serena sold her to
a Spanish merchant who restored her to her former
sleekness and put her to work transporting goods
throughout the Mediterranean.

She plied this trade faithfully for many years,

before succumbing to the ravages of age and labor. When she had outlived her usefulness, she was sailed to Barcelona and sold to a salvager for scrap. Picked apart, she sat at the dock a rotting hulk with no masts or spars or rigging, unloved and forgotten. During an especially bad winter in 1565, her hull was broken up and used as firewood.

She had never lived and therefore could not die, and in the end, no one mourned her passing. But like all sailing ships she was so lifelike that she seemed to have her own spirit, personality, and life force. And when she was broken up and burned as firewood, the space she had formerly occupied became vacant, which is a sign of death. Her destruction should have been mourned if only by the little humans she bore safely across the ocean sea to the Indies.

Orocobix did not give up easily on his belief in God Carlos. He retrieved the cuirass from the bottom of the river and brought it to his bohio, where he painted it with shapes and figures he had seen in a dream, and it became his most treasured zemi.

He stubbornly maintained to all the tribe that Carlos has been resurrected, and when Calliou and Colibri swore that the invaders were men and not gods, he strongly disagreed.

At first, the elders did not know what to believe, and so things might have stayed as they were except for a discovery Calliou made a few weeks later when a body washed up on the shore, which turned out to have been the boy Alonzo who had been so carelessly buried at sea. There was no mistaking the body for an Arawak's, and to make his grisly point unmistakably clear, Calliou lugged it to the village so that all could see a dead god.

Nonetheless, as Orocobix grew older, his memories of God Carlos became mythic and sacred. Every time he told the god's story he enriched it with such lavish details that it soon became weighted down and cryptic like the Catholic liturgy. Tribesmen cringed and hurried out of earshot if they thought he was about to recite it. Yet he was so respected as a holy man that on the death of Ganiquo, the shaman, Orocobix was named his replacement. In this capacity he prayed many times to various zemis to save his people, but there was no heavenly thunderbolt, no intervention, nothing but the hideously indifferent silence of heaven.

Orocobix lived a long life and saw repeated proof that the men from the sky were not gods, nor spiritual, nor anything more than greedy, wicked men. He witnessed their ravaging of his tribe, and in various skirmishes with the Spaniards, he inflicted wounds on their soldiers, some of which caused death. Yet he clung to the myth of God Carlos to the bitter end. His people forgave him this obsession, and he rose so high in their esteem that upon becoming a feeble and sick old man, he was honored by the elders with death by strangulation as he slept.

To escape the predations of the Spaniards, the entire tribe, when Orocobix was still alive, moved into the deep mountainous interior of the island, setting up a village at the headwaters of the White River. Today the site, located in the mountainous district of St. Ann's marked on the map as Bellevue, is one of the best preserved Arawak middens or garbage dumps in Jamaica, and anthropological excavations have yielded many artifacts and shards of pottery that tell of the life and death of a once flourishing people.

De la Serena returned to his family in Majorca and settled down into the community where he became known as a pious man who was always a good choice for leading public prayer. He grew old and died still fixed in his belief that Mount de la Serena towered over Jamaica. It did not. A scribe in the cartography office threw out *Mount de la Serena* and reinstated the simpler *Blue Mountain* because the young King Charles had expressed his displeasure with the recent ornateness of Spanish place names. De la Serena went to his grave unaware that no feature of the New World bore the imprint of his name.

Old Hernandez went back to sea until he was truly too old for the work of a seafarer and retired to the countryside where he lived to an ancient age honored by his family and friends.

* * *

Calliou and Colibri both died in battle against the Spaniards.

The cacique, Datijao, was lured into a trap by the Spaniards, who invited him to a peace talk—a common ploy used by the invader. When he arrived, the Spaniards seized him and threatened him with hanging as an example to his people unless he converted to Catholicism. A priest gravely warned him that his soul would go to hell if he were hanged.

Datijao asked, "And where do the souls of Spaniards go?"

"To heaven."

"I prefer an afterlife without Spaniards," the cacique said quietly.

They hanged him.

The boy Pedro did not intend to tell anyone about what had really happened to Carlos, but he was badly in need of a father and tended to gravitate toward any man who paid him attention. Over the course of the voyage home, he dogged the footsteps of Monsieur, following him throughout the ship wherever he went.

Monsieur embodied the appetites and idiosyncratic ways of the stereotypical Frenchman. He ended every day by drinking wine heavily and always went to bed drunk. One night, he persuaded Pedro to have some wine, which made the boy tipsy and dizzy. It also made him chatty, and as the *Santa Inez* ghosted under the stars, he told Monsieur what had really happened to Carlos.

When the boy was finished with his story, Monsieur exclaimed sympathetically that it was the most moving tale he'd ever heard. He was in his cups and began to sob loudly and made such a commotion that the night watch wandered over to see what was wrong. Eventually, after much sniffling, Monsieur lay out on the deck of the *Santa Inez* and fell asleep.

Some days later, as the *Santa Inez* was approaching the Canary Islands, Monsieur was working on a final draft of his map when he remembered the story the boy had told and was so moved again that he impulsively named a bluff on the Jamaican south coast Pedro Bluff and the bay beneath, Pedro Bay. He did this on his own without telling anyone.

The same scribe who had erased the name *Mount de la Serena* from the map because he thought it clumsy, left *Pedro Bluff* untouched because his sister had just given birth to her first child whom she also named Pedro. Over four hundred years after the voyage of the *Santa Inez*, the names Pedro Bluff and Pedro Bay still exist on maps of Jamaica.

Monsieur soon disappeared from the stage, for his was a nomadic spirit that would wander the rounded earth over his lifetime, mapping it. If his theory is correct, by now he would have outlived twenty generations, assumed dozens of nationalities, had scores of wives, and fathered thousands of children. Otherwise, muttering the last words, "I do not agree with this," he has gone to the place that all men go when their years are spent.

The boy Pedro returned to his childhood village in the Pyrénées, where he grew into a good man who was especially gentle and kindly with women. He never found out that a part of Jamaica had been named after him, just as the people who live today on Pedro Bluff have no idea that its name was inspired by a Spanish cabin boy who visited the island briefly in 1520.

Is this account of the voyage of the *Santa Inez* true? And what does it mean? In this confused world where truth and meaning are dark and unknowable, it is as good a truth as any.

As Colibri, the hummingbird, said in a moment of wisdom, "There is no truth. There is only explanation."

Also available from Akashic Books

THE DUPPY
a novel by Anthony C. Winkler
186 pages, trade paperback, $13.95

"*The Duppy* is the outrageously funny and often insightful brainchild of Anthony C. Winkler."
—*Jamaica Gleaner*

"Jamaican-born novelist Winkler recounts the journey of Taddeus Augustus Baps, a 47-year-old Jamaican man who becomes a 'duppy,' or spirit, after he dies . . . Baps befriends God, bickers with a conflicted American philosopher and travels in an effort to expand his otherworldly horizons. Winkler (*Dog War*) earns a lot of chuckles as he pokes fun at cultural stereotypes and the afterlife."
—*Publishers Weekly*

THE LUNATIC
a novel by Anthony C. Winkler
252 pages, trade paperback, $15.95

"By far the funniest book I've read in a decade, although its ribald atmosphere is sprayed with the pepper-gas of aggressive social satire."
—*Washington Post Book World*

"*The Lunatic* is a small masterpiece and should not be missed."
—*ForeWord*

"*The Lunatic* is a brilliantly written and outrageous Jamaican fable."
—*Jamaica Gleaner*

DOG WAR
a novel by Anthony C. Winkler
194 pages, trade paperback original, $14.95

"Winkler applies his wicked sensibility to immigrant experience in Florida . . . He has a fine ear for patois and dialogue, and a love of language that makes bawdy jokes crackle."
—*New Yorker*

"*Dog War* offers an amusing glance at America through an immigrant's eye, a breezy treat to keep you company on the beach at Montego Bay or, perhaps, your local dog park."
—*Entertainment Weekly*

KINGSTON NOIR
edited by Colin Channer
288 pages, trade paperback original, $15.95

Brand-new stories by: Marlon James, Kwame Dawes, Patricia Powell, Chris Abani, Colin Channer, Marcia Douglas, Leone Ross, Kei Miller, Christopher John Farley, Ian Thomson, and Thomas Glave.

From Trench Town to Half Way Tree to Norbrook to Portmore and beyond, the stories of *Kingston Noir* shine light into the darkest corners of this fabled city. Together, the outstanding tales in *Kingston Noir* comprise the best volume of short fiction ever to arise from the literary wellspring that is Jamaica.

CERVANTES STREET
a novel by Jaime Manrique
320 pages, hardcover: $24.95, trade paperback: $15.95

"A sprawling vivacious big-hearted novel. Manrique is fantastically talented and this is perhaps his masterpiece."
—Junot Díaz, author of *The Brief Wondrous Life of Oscar Wao*

"Cervantes like we've never known him: the rogue, the lover, the soldier, the slave, and above all, the poet. In this novel, Jaime Manrique reminds us that the great writer was a man of flesh and blood whose eventful life seemed destined for great literature."
—Esmeralda Santiago, author of *Conquistadora*

JOHN CROW'S DEVIL
a novel by Marlon James
232 pages, trade paperback, $15.95

"A powerful first novel . . . Writing with assurance and control, James uses his small-town drama to suggest the larger anguish of a postcolonial society struggling for its own identity."
—*New York Times* (Editors' Choice)

"First novelist James moves effortlessly between lyrical patois and trenchant observations . . . It's 150-proof literary rum guaranteed to intoxicate and enchant. Highly recommended."
—*Library Journal* (starred review)